JUDGE HARTWELL

A MEREDITH, MASSACHUSETTS NOVEL

J.A. McINTOSH

Visit our website at **www.StillwaterPress.com** for more information.

First Stillwater River Publications Edition

ISBN: 978-1-950339-92-1

1 2 3 4 5 6 7 8 9 10
Written by J.A. McIntosh
Published by Stillwater River Publications, Pawtucket, RI, USA.

This is a work of fiction. All of the characters, events, places, and organizations in this novel are products of the author's imagination or are used ficticiously.

The views and opinions expressed in this book are solely those of the author and do not necessarily reflect the views and opinions of the publisher.

To my parents, William J. and Marilyn P. McIntosh.

Thanks for everything.

To P G

It's dedicated to
you

J W M I

WEDNESDAY

I'M A VISUAL PERSON AND I DIDN'T LIKE WHAT I WAS SEEING.

The court officers sauntered into my courtroom and stood in front of all three exits. Two older men stood stiffly at attention, one by the main courtroom door and one by the prisoner entrance. Cally, my favorite, stood by the exit to the judge's lobby. All three scanned the room.

Niagara Fontaine, attorney for the Massachusetts Department of Children and Families, was objecting to the evidence being introduced by the mother's counsel. My replacement clerk, Robert, couldn't find the evidence stickers to put on the document. He was opening and closing drawers under his desk. One advantage of sitting at the judge's raised bench, I can see everything that is going on in the courtroom. Robert stopped playing with the desk drawers and Attorney Fontaine stopped talking when Cally approached me on the bench.

"Cally, what's going on? Why all the court officers?"

"Judge Hartwell, we have a situation." Cally adjusted his belt. "Everyone needs to remain in the courtroom until it's settled."

Gerard Paoletti, the mother's lawyer, stood up and looked around the room. Attorney Margorie Warner, for the children, remain seated.

"Are we in danger?" asked Attorney Warner.

"No, ma'am." Cally was always polite. "We just need you to stay here until we resolve the matter." Cally turned to me. "Judge, are these all the people involved in this matter? Has anyone left the courtroom in the last half hour?"

I looked around the room. Jenna, my regular clerk, hadn't showed for work that morning. Her replacement, Robert, sat in front of me. The mother's therapist was on the witness stand. Attorney Paoletti sat at the table to my right and Attorney Warner, Attorney Fontaine, and the social worker at the table to my left, with the mother sitting, huddled, by the back door.

"The probation officer left about ten minutes ago, to run a criminal record check on the mother's boyfriend. Other than that, we've all been here since the hearing started, about forty-five minutes ago," I said.

"Anybody else in or out?" asked Cally.

"I don't think so," I said. "It's a light day, not many people around."

Cally nodded and took up his position at the door.

My phone vibrated across the bench in front of me. I glanced down at the screen as it lit up with a message from my daughter. *I can't find my ballet shoes.* I suppressed the urge to tell her I didn't have them with me in the courtroom.

A video monitor, connected to the courthouse surveillance system, stood on the court officer's desk. I got off the bench, walked to his work station, and looked at the monitors. Security personnel were turning back people trying to enter the courthouse. The corridor was empty. A small crowd gathered in the parking garage. No help there.

I went back to the bench. My phone danced around my desk.

Another text from my daughter about her ballet shoes. *Where did you have them last?* I texted back, inadvertently knocking over the stack of mail piled precariously on my desk. The top letter was addressed "Dear Amythyst Basil," as if I were an old friend. I went by A.B., or Abbi, and was an expert in avoiding my given name. I threw the letter in the trashcan under the bench.

Court officers continued to stand by the exits. What was going on?

Cally's microphone, attached to his left shoulder, crackled. He had a brief conversation with the person on the other end and conferred with the other officers. Cally took a few steps toward me. "Judge, we are asking that all non-court personnel

leave the building. Folks, you will be required to show photo identification as you go."

Bert Rodgers, the court officer by the back door, escorted the parties in my case out of the courtroom. Attorneys Paoletti, Fontaine, and Warner followed him.

I looked at Robert, my sessions clerk, and Cally, and the other court officer, who I did not recognize. I knew all the juvenile court officers; he must have come from District Court. The four of us didn't take up much space in the large courtroom.

"I guess we wait," said Robert.

My phone vibrated again. *Dad says we need to go to ballet class NOW and I don't have my shoes.* I couldn't be bothered with the shoes right now. *If your dad's there, have him look for them.* I responded and jabbed my finger to turn off the phone. Of course, now they'll both be mad at me.

"Damn Magda," I said.

"Isn't Magda a woman's name?" whispered Cally.

Magda was my husband's name, but U. S. residents often

mistook it for a woman's name. I smiled at Cally's lame attempt at humor, but I had other things on my mind.

"Cally, what the hell is going on?" I drummed my fingers on my desk.

Cally turned his back and conferred with someone, using the microphone attached to his uniform. I couldn't make out the words.

Cally turned to face me. "Judge, we found a body in the parking garage under the courthouse."

"A body? Somebody died there?" The parking garage was for the cars of judges and court personnel. Nobody got in without a pass. Of course, that didn't stop people from walking into the garage.

"Yes, Judge." Cally swallowed loudly. "The body's been identified."

I realized he must know the person who died. I probably did too.

"Who is it?" I asked.

"There's no easy way to say this." Cally adjusted his belt again. "It's your clerk, Jenna Jay."

My clerk, Jenna. An hour ago, I'd been fuming because she hadn't showed up for work and hadn't called. Then they assigned me Robert, as a temporary, and he didn't know the procedures or where anything was. While I was bitching about the inconvenience to me, Jenna was dead in the garage.

I held back my tears. It didn't look good when the judge cried, even though I'd only been a judge for about six months. I realized I had stopped breathing and was clutching my pen so hard that my knuckles were white.

"I have no other details, Judge." Cally spoke softly and avoided my eyes. Jenna was his friend too.

"This is awful," I said. "Has anyone told Chloe?"

I'd know Jenna for over two years and her wife, Chloe, was in my study group at college. I imagined Jenna and Chloe at their wedding and trying to deal with their rescue dog, Max. And tried not to think of her dead in the parking garage.

"I don't know, Judge," said Cally. "It's being taken care of by the state police."

"The state police? Why the state police?" I didn't believe Cally's assertion he didn't know more than he was telling. He knew everything that went on in the courthouse.

"They suspect homicide," said Cally. "There's all kinds of rumors, but that's all I know right now."

"Homicide? Who would want to kill Jenna?" I asked. The tears were piling up in the corner of my eyes. Oh, hell. A few escaped and started down my cheeks.

Cally handed me a tissue and then looked down at the floor. "She made me cookies for my birthday last week. And now she's dead."

"That's what I mean. She remembered everybody's birthday and organized all the holiday parties. Why would someone want to kill her?"

Bert Rodgers returned to the courtroom. "All non-court personnel have been escorted from the building," he said. "I've been asked to get the best numbers to contact you, and then you're free to go." He stopped when he saw me. "Judge, are you okay?"

I wiped my eyes. "No, I'm not. I just need a few minutes to deal with this."

"You've been freed to go," Bert repeated. "But I can wait a few minutes while you get your things together. I'll see you out of the building. And I have to ask that you not discuss this matter with anyone else until the police have talked to you."

"How can I discuss this matter with anyone else? I don't know anything." I picked up my phone and mail from the desk.

Bert escorted me to the office where I got my briefcase. I started to pick up the pile of casefiles on my desk, but left them. I'd deal with them later. I thought of calling Chloe but decided against it. I was a coward and didn't want to be the one to tell her Jenna was dead.

I reconsidered my decision about calling Chloe on my way home. Maybe she needed to hear the news from me, not the police. No, I'm dangerous when I use a cellphone in the car. That visual processing thing again. If I'm distracted from what I was seeing, even on Bluetooth, I can't even drive straight. Besides, the police would make sure she had someone there with her.

I pulled into the driveway and pushed the remote on the garage door. It creaked open; another thing that should be looked at. I drove forward but stopped short when I spotted Phillip's mountain bike in the center of the garage. Three kids and they had to park their toys on my half of the garage. Not exactly children anymore. Ashroff was going to graduate from high school this year and the twins, Phillip and Pamela, were in ninth grade. But still they left their stuff in my space and expected me to pick it up. I got out, moved Phillip's bicycle, and pulled into the garage. The garage door opened directly into the kitchen.

At three p.m. on a Wednesday, my kitchen was full. My husband and Pam had just arrived home.

"I don't want to take ballet lessons anymore." Pam dropped her bag and purse on the table. I didn't see any ballet shoes in the bag.

Phillip and his friends were in the kitchen, celebrating the freedom of school vacation week. Ashroff sat at the kitchen table.

"If you put things away in the same place every time, you wouldn't need to search for them at the last minute," said Ashroff.

Pam stared at him.

Ashroff, my oldest, had the long, oval face of my husband, Magda. Phillip looked like me, with a heart-shaped face and chestnut hair. Pam, Phillip's fourteen-year-old twin, was our changeling. She had black, curly hair and a bubbly personality in a family of deliberate thinkers.

"Honey, did you get the milk and eggs?" My husband, Magda, did not even look at me as he spoke.

"No." I forgot I was supposed to stop at the market. "I need to talk to you. Alone."

Magda's head came up at that request. I tried to remember the last time we were alone together other than in the bedroom. With his long hours at the family business, and my spending all day at the courthouse, it had been months. Magda turned and left the kitchen and I followed him into the office.

The office used to be a sunroom and its glass walls overlooked the garden, just turning green in the April drizzle. At least, some sprouts had appeared before the gray days. The room contained two desks, his and hers, of equal size. That had been one of the first fights when we bought the house. Magda expected to have a home office. I'd had to fight for equal space. I won that battle, not that I got to reap the spoils very often. I closed the door after us.

"I got some bad news today."

Magda came over and put his arm around me. "What happened?"

His sympathy was too much for me. I started to cry.

Where I was good at silence, Magda was the master. It hung heavy in the room. If I spoke the words about Jenna's death, it would become real.

I crossed over to my desk and stood behind it. "Jenna was found dead in the courthouse. Murdered." I took a deep breath. "I thought about calling Chloe but I decided to let someone else tell her that Jenna was dead. But I need to go see her."

"Of course you do," said Magda.

"I may be there a while, depending on what she needs," I continued. "Will you feed the children and make sure Phillip gets to soccer practice?"

I sensed, rather than saw, Magda shift into a defensive position. "I need to get back to the factory. The stamping machine has broken down and I need to reschedule deliveries."

"Magda, Jenna is dead. I need to be there."

"The children and I need you. You are supposed to take care of us." He wasn't arguing, he was stating what he considered to be an obvious fact. "You can go later."

"If Chloe asks me, I'll go. The kids can eat peanut butter and jelly sandwiches and Phillip can miss soccer."

Magda leaned back against the door casing. "We need a housekeeper."

"I don't have time for this now," I said. Like I didn't have time for it the four hundred and sixteen other times we'd discussed a housekeeper. "You and the children will need to adapt."

"Adapt? Is that what we must do, adapt? I hired a housekeeper for you. You fired the housekeeper because she doesn't do things the way you want. Then you complain because you do what the housekeeper, who isn't here, can't. Someone needs to run the house, and, by your own choice, it is you."

I couldn't believe we were having this conversation decades into the twenty-first century. And not for the first time. I was responsible for the house. He would hire help, but I was still responsible. I shook my head.

"It's school vacation. If I need to, I can send the children to be with my mother." I hated myself for offering solutions that did not address the fact I wanted Magda to take on housekeeping responsibilities.

"Why do you want to send the kids to see her? All she has been trying to do for twenty years is split us up. If they spend time with her, that's all she'll talk about."

He had a point. My mother still couldn't believe that I met and married an Arab. I pointed out to her that although his parents were born in Egypt, he was a Christian, a Coptic Christian, born in Worcester, Massachusetts. It didn't matter. According to my mother, he was not a real Christian nor a real citizen.

"I guess we muddle through like we always do," I said.

Magda smiled. "It's what we are good at." He came over and put his arms around me.

"Muddling through" was our mantra. Early in our marriage, I'd tried to schedule our life. When we'd buy a house, when we'd have kids, when we'd be financially secure. Magda had looked at my pages and pages of notes and shrugged. We'd been trying to strike a balance for years.

"I'm tired," I said, though I didn't leave his arms. It felt good there. "So what do you suggest we do? Hire another housekeeper?"

"We can't keep hiring housekeepers and letting them go. The agency will think that we are bad clients." Magda stepped back, but kept hold of my hand. "It goes on the record as being unstable."

I thought for a moment. "What if we hire cleaners to come in once a month? And maybe someone to make meals that can be frozen?"

"Sounds like a plan," said Magda. "Why don't you look into that?"

There it was again. Housekeeping was my job.

"As for tonight," continued Magda. "I'll have Ash take Phillip to soccer."

I must be frazzled. I hadn't thought of that.

My beeper went off just as Magda and I got to the bottom of the stairs. Magda stopped.

"I have to take this." I stepped into our office and dialed the number on the display.

"State Police Barracks. Trooper Manetti."

I glanced up at the clock. 4:25. On top of everything else, I was now the on-call judge for the evening.

"Judge Hartwell. You paged me?"

"Yes, ma'am. Got a lady here who needs an Abuse Prevention Order."

"Put her on."

A definite male voice came on the phone. "Judge Hartwell?"

"This is the judge. Do you require an abuse prevention order?"

"Judge, this is Gerard Paoletti. My client has been beaten up by her husband and needs a restraining order immediately."

"Please put me on speaker phone. I need to talk to your client."

"She's pretty shook up. I can assure you she needs help."

"Is she on her way to the hospital?"

"No, she refused medical attention. She just needs the order."

Attorney Paoletti knew this wasn't the way it was done. To get an Abuse Prevention Order under Massachusetts General Laws,

Chapter 209A, the person asking for it must make a statement under oath. As the phone made signing an affidavit impossible, I needed to talk to the woman. Maybe she was upset and he was being protective of her.

"You know that's not the procedure. Please put your client on the phone."

"She isn't in any condition to talk. Being asked questions will only make it worse."

Now I was being accused of messing up the lives of people I hadn't even met yet. Attorney Paoletti was a strong advocate for his client, but he knew the rules.

"I need a statement from the victim. Without that, I can't allow the order to issue."

Gerard Paoletti made a growl deep in his throat. As if this call had inconvenienced him more than it did me. He put the woman on the phone.

"I need an Abuse Prevention Order." The woman's voice was low but it was clear.

"Please tell me what happened."

"My husband hit me. He threw the phone at me and I have a bruise on my head." This delivered in a monotone.

In the background, I heard Paoletti say, "You need to tell her that you're afraid of him."

The woman echoed him. "I'm afraid of him."

She said the right words. Trauma affected people in different ways. Maybe she coped by convincing herself it wasn't a problem. And I needed to get the hell off the phone. "Order granted until court opens at nine o'clock tomorrow morning. Please discuss with the trooper what you need to do to extend the order beyond tomorrow." I hung up.

Magda stood in the doorway. He didn't look like he was going to move. I squeezed past him, ducked out through the garage, and was in my car before he could catch up with me. I pushed the remote control for the door as I started the car and I was in the street before he got a word out of his mouth.

I escaped but with nowhere to go. My home was not a refuge and the courthouse reminded me that Jenna was dead. My mobile phone pinged. I pulled over into a local park and looked at the text from my daughter. *Where are you?* The on-call beeper buzzed. I threw them both on the seat and got out of the car.

The park was a local hangout. A couple of acres with a kiddie play area and a pond in the middle. I headed toward the pond and crossed the wooden bridge. At the highest point in the arch of the bridge, I stopped at the benches placed there and sat down. It had stopped raining but the air was still gray and chilly.

I stared over the pond. When in hell had I been put in charge of everything? I was responsible for judicial decisions, family decisions, children decisions, and house decisions. Magda was right, some of it was of my own making. I had been sure I could do it all. And I was so certain I could do it perfectly. Well, damn it, I can't.

A buzzing sound interrupted my self-pity and I saw a tall, thin man riding on an electric scooter. He had dark hair and wore a hoodie and sweatpants. He stopped his scooter near me. I looked around. Nobody in the park but us. I stood up.

"You don't have to leave on my account," he said. "My name's Richard."

He raised his head. His left eye was black and blue.

"I've got to go." I pulled the flaps of my coat around me. It was not made for this weather; it was a light coat I left in the car.

"Why're you sitting out here in the rain when you got

someplace else to go?"

"It's not raining," I said with a slight edge in my voice. "I needed to take a break."

"We all need a break sometimes," he said. "Call me if you need to talk." He pulled a business card from an inside pocket on his coat and held it out to me face-side up so that I could read it. I studied him for a second. He didn't look over thirty, but he handled the business card like a pro. *Richard Paoletti, Citizen Advocacy,* I read the card, with a local address. I looked back up at him with interest. He smiled and turned to leave.

"Hey," I called out. "Are you related to Attorney Paoletti?"

"He's my dad." He paused and sat up straighter on the scooter. "Don't hold it against me."

"Didn't know he had a son."

"Yeah, well, he wanted a baseball player. He got me." Richard gestured toward the scooter. "I've got a heart condition. Makes it hard to walk."

"I'm sorry," I said.

"Don't be sorry." He had a disarming smile, even with the black eye. "Makes me non-threatening. All the women talk to me."

I stuffed the card in my coat pocket. "I really do have to get going. Have a good day."

When I got back to the car, I picked up the phone and the beeper I had left on the seat. The phone showed three calls, all from the same local number. The beeper had two entries. Barely an hour since the last call, this was going to be a busy night. Was it a full moon? Cally, the court officer, swore it was crazier during a full moon. I think it's just crazy.

I felt the guilt I had been managing to keep at bay. What if the state police had tried to reach me while I was ignoring the phone? What if Chloe needed me?

The numbers on my caller ID were random, I didn't recognize any of them. I listened to all the messages and breathed a sigh of relief. All three were from the courthouse, asking me to call. The court phone system went through the internet, so phone numbers were listed from all over the state. I glanced at my watch. Too late, the court was closed now.

As I stared at my phone, it rang again. I answered it immediately. Trooper DePaul asked me to come down to the police station, to be interviewed about Jenna. I told him I didn't know much, but he insisted I needed to be interviewed in person. He said he was free now. I headed toward the police station to get it over with.

I still hadn't called Chloe. By now, she knew of Jenna's death and so I didn't have that excuse not to call. I'd contact her as soon as I left the police station.

The Meredith Police Station was a modern, faux brick building on Main Street. The original plans called for a flat roof, but trusses were added as an afterthought to give it a slight pitch. Anyone who lived through a New England winter knew that a flat roof was a bad idea. Although the added roof height served the purpose, it gave the building a slightly off-balance look.

Heat hit me when I opened the front door.

The waiting room was tiny, with a rack on the wall containing pamphlets about substance abuse treatment and battered women's services. A locked box for the disposal of unused medications. On the opposite wall were doors to the bathrooms and one interview room. A receptionist sat behind the bullet-proof glass at the end. I signed in and she left to announce my arrival.

My phone beeped. Magda this time. *"When will you be home?"* I told him I was at the police station and it would be a while.

A man who looked no older than my son Phillip came to the door. He was wearing a blue uniform, so I guessed he was at least old enough to have graduated from high school.

"Please come with me," he said, and held the door open for me.

I walked beside him down a corridor with doors on both sides. Dull silver plates attached to the wall beside the doors identified a common room, an evidence room, and a sergeant's office. A hand-written sign taped to one door announcing "Fingerprint scanner down again!" lent some humanity to the otherwise bureaucratic hallway.

The young officer opened a door to the right marked "conference room" and silently bid me to enter. The room furnishings consisted of a long table and an array of cushioned chairs. At least it wasn't an interrogation room. A poster on the wall had the numbers for the Fire Department and the Department of Children and Families, both the Leominster and the Worcester offices. An older man, clean-shaven but with his fair hair falling over his face, gestured towards a chair and asked me to sit down.

"I'm Trooper DePaul," he said. "Would you like anything to drink, Judge Hartwell?"

The young man who escorted me into the office looked taken aback. I assumed by the look that nobody told him I was a judge.

"No thanks. I just want to get this over with." I put my purse on the table. My phone beeped again.

"Do you need to get that?" asked Trooper DePaul.

I pulled my phone from my purse and looked at it briefly before setting it on the table. "No, but I'm going to keep it on.

I'm the on-call judge this evening." I looked up at the trooper. "Are you in charge of the investigation?"

"Yes, ma'am. The local police are helping us out."

I knew that before I asked the question but I was trying to calm my nerves for what was coming next. In a town the size of Meredith, any murder investigation would be run by the State Police. That left the question of why he wanted to talk to me. I asked him.

"Well, ma'am, you work with Ms. Jay every day. When was the last time you saw her?"

I took me a minute to think back. My last thoughts about Jenna were that she didn't show for work this morning and she had inconvenienced me and stuck me with the temporary clerk, Robert. Not going to dwell there.

"I last spoke to Jenna about four thirty yesterday. We had some tea, talked about rescheduling cases and our mothers."

Trooper DePaul reached up to scratch his neck. "Your mothers?"

"Yes, we are both dealing with elderly mothers and that can sometimes be difficult."

My phone beeped again. I picked it up and it said private call. DePaul watched and waited. I put it down. "Is there anything else?"

"Yes, Judge. What was Jenna Jay's mood when you spoke to her?"

"Pensive."

"Pensive."

I'm a judge; I don't answer questions that haven't been asked yet. And that wasn't a question. Chatting is not in my nature or training.

"Listen, Judge." The trooper moved his chair closer to mine, as if we were going to have a confidential conversation. "Did you and Ms. Jay have an argument?"

"No."

"Cally, the court officer, said that you and Ms. Jay were arguing in the parking garage yesterday."

"Arguing?" I was baffled. I didn't remember any argument.

"Yes, ma'am. Cally said that you and Ms. Jay were arguing about her missing work. It appeared that Ms. Jay was trying to get away from you."

I thought back to our conversation of the day before. I remembered the quiet moment over tea, talking about our lives. The discussion in the parking garage took all of two minutes, earlier in the day. "Ms. Jay has been absent three times in the past two weeks," I said. "I was worried about her. She's never missed a day in over three years. I asked her if something was wrong."

"And what did she say?"

I looked directly at Trooper DePaul. "She said nothing was wrong and I didn't need to worry about it. Then she attempted to leave. That must be what Cally saw." I hesitated. "I didn't believe that nothing was wrong and pressed her on it."

"What did she say?"

"She repeated that everything was fine and went back to work."

The trooper made some notes on the pad in front of him.

"I need to go see Chloe and my family is waiting for me." I stood up. "Is there anything else?"

"You know Chloe Jay, the wife?"

"Chloe and I met in college, over twenty years ago. I've known her longer than I've known Jenna."

"Did you and Jenna ever have a relationship? Or you and Chloe?"

"No." I wasn't going to elaborate.

"No jealousy? No spurned lover?" Trooper DePaul was very good at asking questions like he didn't care about the answers.

"No. I introduced Chloe to Jenna. They've been married two years and seem very happy."

"How would you characterize their relationship? Other than happy?"

I felt my lips curve into a smile at the thought of Chloe and Jenna together. Probably not a good look for a police station. I frowned. "Jenna was a free spirit. She was social and she could and would talk to anybody. I had some reservations about keeping her as my clerk when I became a judge, but she worked out well."

Trooper DePaul made a note on his pad. "What kind of reservations did you have?"

It took me a moment to think back to the time I hired her. "As I said, she is very social but not a good organizer. When I set up the plan for my courtroom, she followed it willingly. And her social skills often made difficult situations easier. I tend to be more abrupt."

"And her relationship with her wife?" asked the trooper.

"Chloe is an elementary school principal and super organized. She lent the structure at home, like I did at work. Jenna and Chloe decided not to have children at this time because they wanted to spend time with each other." I didn't tell him that Jenna often said that children would upset Chloe's well-organized life.

DePaul leaned over the table. "And what was your relationship with the women as a couple?"

I pushed back in my chair, away from him. "I'm friends with

both of them. As I told you, Chloe and I met in college. When Jenna came to work for me, I introduced them. It worked out."

Trooper DePaul made some more notes and then he stood up. "I may have some more questions for you, at a later date. Are you planning to stay in town?"

"I sometimes go to visit my mother in Keene, New Hampshire. You have my contact information." I left.

My phone rang as I made the right at the end of the street. I refused to answer it, upset and driving. If it was important, whoever it was could call the state police. If they convinced the trooper it warranted a call, the state police contacted me. Even with a wireless set-up, I didn't use the phone in the car.

I pulled into my driveway again. Phillip's mountain bike was back in the middle of the garage. I couldn't pull in. It shouldn't bother me so much, but it did.

As I entered the kitchen, heavy footsteps clomped on the floor. Phillip entered the room. When did my son get so tall and walk so heavily?

"What's for dinner?" he asked.

"I've got some frozen chicken for kabobs and some left-over baba ghanoush," I said. "I'll see if I can find some vegetables for a salad. We'll have something in about forty-five minutes." Dinner I could control, even if other parts of my life weren't going well.

I walked into the pantry to get the chicken out of the freezer. And tripped over Pamela's ballet slippers.

We managed to have a decent meal together. Just the family tonight, no friends of the kids or people from work. I don't know this, but it seemed like Magda told the kids to show up and not act up, as I had a rough day. I don't remember much of it. It could have been the two glasses of wine I had, or it could have been the crash after dealing with Jenna's death.

I still hadn't called Chloe. No time like the present.

The phone rang six times before it was answered.

"Abbi?" Chloe's voice was low and rough. She was an elementary school principal, usually decisive and in charge.

"Chloe, I'm so sorry."

"I know, that's what everyone says." I heard her take a drink and swallow. "I'm glad you called."

"Are you taking care of yourself?" I wanted to scream at her, take care of yourself, but managed to make it into a question.

"Yeah, it's been tough. The police just left." She started to cry.

"Are you a suspect?" I knew she was a suspect, just because she was the surviving spouse. "Do you need a lawyer?"

"I don't need a lawyer," said Chloe. "But I do need a friend who gives good advice."

"Do you want me to come over? I could be there in about twenty minutes."

Magda came in as I was making the last statement and mouthed "where are you going?"

I heard Chloe take a deep breath. "I miss her so much. I look around and see her stuff and think she's going to come home at any minute."

"Chloe, I want to help you. What can I do?"

"There have been so many people in and out of the house today. I just want to be alone." I heard the clicking of nails and a bark. "Of course, Max is here with me. I'll just talk to him and go to bed." Max barked again. "But I would like to talk to you about something. In person, not over the phone. Can you come over tomorrow? Early?"

"Is there something wrong? Does this have anything to do

with Jenna missing work lately?"

"I really don't want to go into this now." Chloe did sound exhausted. "Can we talk in the morning? Before you go to court?"

"I'll be there at eight for breakfast." I said. I rearranged my morning schedule in my head. I would be at the courthouse by ten thirty "I'll bring coffee and pastry, so you don't need to prepare anything."

"See you then." Max barked again and Chloe terminated the call.

The children had all made plans to go out that night. Ash was taking Phillip to soccer practice. Pam insisted on going also and they were going to meet up with friends afterward. We waved them off with strict instructions to be back by 10:00 p.m., at the latest

Magda and I snuggled on the couch to watch the seven o'clock news. We'd no more than settled in when the phone rang again.

"Don't answer it," said Magda.

"It's Dale," I said. "I have to answer it."

Magda sat up. I missed his arms around me. "I know it's Dale. I just don't like you talking to him. It's just weird."

"Dale has called every Wednesday and Saturday for the last six months. If I ignore him, he'll just call back." I picked up my phone.

"Just checking in," Dale never said hello. "Your mother is as cranky as ever, so I guess she's feeling well."

"How did the visit with the doctor go?" I asked.

"About as well as can be expected. Told him I was her care-taker and he looked at me funny. Then asked about my latest book." Dale and my mother had a working relationship. He took care of her and she edited his books. Though she had mobility issues, her mind was as sharp as ever. It seemed to be working out, as they'd managed to live together for the last six months. That wasn't easy with my mother.

"The doctor wanted to put her on blood thinners and she refused again. I threatened to call her daughter, Abbi, with the health care proxy, and make her take them."

"And how did that work out?" I stood up and started pacing. Magda signaled me to sit down. I ignored him.

"Your mother knows the health care proxy doesn't kick in unless she's incompetent. She's a lot of things, but not incompetent." I heard the clang of metal.

"Are you cooking?" I asked.

"Just making grilled cheese sandwiches," Dale replied. "Need to get some food into your mother before the grad students arrive. I know she'll eat grilled cheese."

"Is she still mentoring grad students? I thought that was over."

"Last meeting tonight. Got to go." Dale hung up without saying good-bye.

I sat back down.

Magda put his arm around me. "How's your mother doing?"

"Still refusing blood thinners. Her Ph.D. is in English, but she knows more about medicine than the doctors." I sighed. "Last meeting of the grad students tonight."

Magda looked at me. "Doesn't Keene State University have a mandatory retirement age? And didn't your mother get there about a decade ago?"

"My mother's only seventy-five. And she only mentors a handful of students a year." I sat up. "And she's good at it, as long as the students come to her. She's still editing Dale's books too."

"Ah, Dale." As in, we're not going to discuss him.

Magda pulled me back into his arms and used the remote to turn on the news. I still loved him. I fell asleep after the weather report.

I woke up when Magda moved his arm.

"Sorry to disturb you," he said. "My arm is falling asleep. Just like you."

I mumbled something. There was a cold place where his arm used to be.

"C'mon, sleepyhead, let's get you to bed." Magda tried to lift me up by my arms.

I protested, looking at the clock on the cable box. "It's just after nine. Too early to go to bed."

"You're exhausted, you need to sleep. At least in bed, I won't have to carry you if you fall asleep." Magda's eyes sparkled, a look I knew well. "Or, if you don't want to sleep, we could find other things to do."

That sounded good, but there was a fifty-fifty chance that I would sleep through it. Either way, I guess bed was a good option.

Magda and I made it up the stairs, performed our nightly routine and climbed into bed. He was naked. I had on my night-gown. Didn't want to appear too eager. And there was still a possibility that I would crash.

Magda put his arms around me and said, "I'm really sorry about Jenna."

I rolled over to face him. "It's been a tough few hours. "

"And our argument didn't help. I'm sorry." He did look sorry.

"I have control issues," he said.

After twenty years of marriage, that wasn't a newsflash. When I first met him, I liked the way he anticipated what I wanted and took care of it. As I got older, it became more annoying. Perhaps because we both thought we were good at the same things.

"Neither of us wants to do the housework," he said. "I have no problem giving it up, but you do. Maybe that's your control issue."

"It's an issue because you want to hire somebody to do the housework but not the work you do."

"We also hire somebody to do the gardening and the lawn maintenance. That's not my thing," he said.

"Yes, but I'm always in charge. It's always my responsibility."

He pulled me closer to him. "Tell me what you want to do, and I'll do it."

I sighed. I couldn't help it. "I don't want to have to ask you. I want you to see the problem and take care of it."

"That's it, isn't it?" He ran his fingers down my arm. "I don't see a problem with a dirty house. Unless we run out of dishes or clothes."

I laughed. Not a full-blown laugh, but a "we've been through this before" laugh.

"So, shall we hire another housekeeper?" Magda asked.

"Or at least someone to do the heavy cleaning," I said. "At least, then we can argue about what she's doing rather than who should be doing the housework."

"There is that." Magda kissed me. I knew him well. And I knew every inch of his body and showed him what I knew.

As I predicted when we went to bed just after nine, I awoke just after eleven. The house was unusually quiet. No kid sounds. If the kids got home at ten, and it was unlikely they got home any sooner, there should be showering sounds and the beeps and clicks as they checked social media. No sound at all.

I stepped into the hallway. The house was dark and quiet. I went to the staircase and peered downstairs; no light down there either. Maybe the kids got home early and were asleep.

I checked the bathroom. Part of the recent renovations was to get a second bathroom for the children. Phillip was always complaining about Pam's hair gel in the shower and her underwear hanging on the towel rack. Nobody was in the bathroom now. And it didn't seem like anybody had been in there recently. No condensation on the mirror and no smell of peppermint or ocean breeze.

I knocked on Pam's door. I pushed it open when I got no answer. The room was dark, and the bed was empty. The digital numbers 11:23 blazed red at her bedside clock. It was out of character for Pam to stay out late and not call us. Maybe her brothers knew where she was.

I crossed the hall to the room shared by Ashroff and Phillip. The weak moonlight showed through the windows. Maybe the gray days had ended. Ashroff's side of the room was immaculate; his books were lined up and all his clothing hung neatly in the closet. His bed was made and empty. My eyes darted to the other side of the room. Amid piles of dirty laundry and things I didn't want to think about, there was a lump in Phillip's bed.

I pushed the lump with my hand and it grunted. Phillip rolled over and peered up at me through squinted eyes. At least one of my children was accounted for.

"What you want?" Phillip did a good imitation of someone roused from a sound sleep.

"I know you're awake." I sat down on the bed beside him. "Where are your brother and sister?"

"Brother and sister?" he parroted me.

"Yes," I said. "How many siblings do you have?"

He tried to roll away from me, but I turned him to face me.

"Last time I saw them they were getting into it." He snorted. "Real bad."

"What do you mean? Getting into it?"

Phillip looked up at the ceiling. I knew all his guises. This was his "I know the answer but don't want to tell you" look.

"It's late. Neither Pam nor Ash are home. You can tell me where they are, or I can start calling people and asking questions." My eyes drilled in on him. "I'll start with your friends, ask them where you were tonight."

Phillip made a quick decision. "Last time I saw them, they were arguing in the middle of Oak Street."

"In the middle of the street?"

"Yeah, on the strip of grass that runs between the east and west side. They were loud."

"Near Joshua's house?" Joshua was a friend of Ash.

Phillip looked up at the ceiling again. "Yeah, near there."

"What were they arguing about?"

"I don't know, Ma. I wasn't really paying attention. Ash wanted Pam to leave and she didn't want to go, or something like that. They tried to pull me into it, so I walked home."

Without a word, I got up from the bed and walked to the door.

"You want me to call them?" Phillip pushed back the covers. Now he wanted to be helpful.

"No, you stay at the house in case they come back. At least I'll know where one of you is. And, if they do come back, you call me immediately."

I left his room, went to mine, and tried both Ash's and Pam's phones. Both went immediately to voicemail. I left text messages for both: *Call me immediately when you get this.* While I was on the phone, Magda woke up. He was instantly alert. I filled him in on the situation. Still no response from either kid. I was still struggling to put on my jeans when he picked up the car keys and asked me if I was ready to go. He was at his best in an emergency. No yelling, no questioning what happened, just go find the kids. While I finished dressing, I filled him in on what Phillip told me.

We got in the car and drove to Oak Street.

THURSDAY

It was a short distance but it seemed like a long drive. We turned onto the street, deserted now except for a cruiser. It sat ominously in the cut-out from the east to the west side of the street. Its flashers weren't on and nobody else was around. Magda parked and got out of the car.

The police officer, hand on his holster, met Magda halfway.

I rolled down my window.

"Can I help you, sir?" The officer took a step closer.

"I'm worried about my children," Magda replied. "They were last seen on this street. They're only fourteen and eighteen years old and were supposed to be home over an hour ago."

"Are you Mr. Amir?"

I got out of the car. At my approach, Magda turned toward me, and the officer again put his hand on his holster.

I started speaking before I got to them. "I'm Judge Hartwell. Do you know where they are?"

The officer glanced at his watch. "About now, somebody down at the station is calling your house."

"Are they injured?" I asked.

"Can I see your identification?" asked the officer, a little awkwardly. "You know, before I give you any more information."

Magda pulled his license out of his wallet and gave it to the officer. The officer looked at me. "Ma'am, your identification?"

"I left the house without my purse or anything else. I was worried."

"Officer, she's my wife," said Magda. "And she's a judge. Please tell us what happened."

The officer stared at the ground for a moment before he spoke. "The girl has some bruises and scratches on her arm where the boy tried to pull her down the street. Other than that, they are both fine." He fingered the license. "Physically."

I started to say something, but stopped myself. If the officer was inclined to give information, I wasn't going to stop him.

"The boy is being charged with assault. Several people saw him try to pull the girl down the street. The girl is a witness but, being a minor, we took her to the station."

"Assault?" asked Magda. "Ash was charged with assault? How did that happen?"

"I'm sorry, sir." The officer looked at the ground again. "That's all the information I can give you." He handed the license back to Magda.

"C'mon, Magda," I said, as I pulled him toward the car. I turned back with one last question for the officer. "Both children are at the Meredith Police Station, correct?"

"Yes, ma'am." I felt him watching us as we walked away and got into the car.

For the second time in twenty-four hours, I walked into the Meredith Police Station. Magda appeared calm and in charge. I was a nervous wreck. I just wanted to see my children and to check for myself that they weren't injured. We could deal with whatever happened.

Magda went up to the glass window that separated him for the nightshift receptionist. He stated his name and his business. He was informed that the bail commissioner was in the building if he wanted to post the payment to get Ashroff released.

I walked up to the window. "I'm Judge Hartwell. Can you help me?"

The receptionist looked at me, with my finger-combed hair and third-best jeans. I didn't look much like a judge. The very same young police officer who I had seen earlier in the day came through the same unmarked door.

"It's okay," he said to the receptionist. "I know who she is, I'll take her to her daughter."

We followed him down the corridor to where Pam sat on a wooden bench. She had a bandage on her right arm but looked otherwise unharmed.

I sat down beside her. "What happened?"

Magda followed the young police officer down the hallway. "Where's my son?"

"He's in a cell," said the officer. "Charged with assault."

"I want to see him." Magda moved closer to the officer.

"Please back up, sir." The officer put his hand on his holster.

I called to my husband, "Magda, come sit down." I patted the hard bench where Pam and I sat.

"Sir, you can't see him until someone pays the bail commissioner."

Magda looked up. "Then let's do that."

"I'll send him out as soon as he is free." The officer opened the door and disappeared into an office.

"Pam, what the hell is going on?" Magda was fast losing his cool.

Pam moved away from Magda and leaned against me. She smelled like beer. Cheap beer.

"Dad, I don't know what happened." Pam started to cry. Her eyes were already red. She'd probably already done a fair share of crying. "I got scratches and a bruise and the cops made a big deal of it."

"What do you mean, you don't know?" Magda moved closer to her.

"Magda, not now." I put my hand on his arm. "We are in the hallway and can be heard by everyone in the station. Let's talk about this after we get home."

I turned to Pam. "Are you alright? Do you need medical care?"

"I'm alright," she said. "Just some scratches where Ash grabbed onto me. The EMT put on some cream and a bandage."

"Okay, we can wait until we get home for the rest of the story," said Magda. He was catching on; he hadn't been married to a lawyer for twenty years for nothing. Anything said here was public and could be used at a trial.

A short, gray-haired man came out of the door that the police officer had disappeared into. He walked quickly but his gray hair and wrinkles indicated he was closer to seventy than fifty. Most bail commissioners were current or retired court employees. I didn't know this man.

"Hello, Mr. Amir, Judge." He nodded to each of us. "I'm Bill Kelleher, the bail commissioner. I heard you wanted to see me."

Magda stood up. "We'd like to take our son home. Now."

Kelleher glanced down at the clip board in his hand, undeterred by Magda's brashness. "I've got all the paperwork here. Just need your signatures and sixty dollars." He looked Magda in the eyes. "Cash only."

Then came the ridiculous spectacle of two adults and a teenager trying to come up with sixty dollars in cash. Magda had forty-five dollars; Pam had a five-dollar bill. I found a five, four ones and a dollar change in my coat pocket. We handed the money to Kelleher, signed the documents, and sat back down to wait. It was cold in the hallway. Pam leaned against me and fell asleep.

About twenty minutes went by. Finally, a police officer escorted Ash into the hallway where we were seated. He had a bloodied lip and was in handcuffs.

Magda got up and rushed toward Ash. "What the hell is going on? Why the handcuffs?"

I hurried up to Magda and put my hand on his arm. "When we get home," I said. "Let's just get everyone out of here."

The police officer handed me a pamphlet. "Your Right to Be Free from Abuse" it read. He took a deep breath and recited the required information. "You can get a restraining order and keep this person away from your family and the victim. If you wish, I can contact the on-call judge and an order can be issued immediately. You will need to appear in court on the next business day to extend the order."

No need to tell him I was the on-call judge that night. "No, thank you," I said.

We left the police station with both our children. Magda drove. Ash sat in the seat behind him. I climbed into the passenger seat and Pam crammed herself against the window in the seat behind me. Nobody said a word on the way home. When we arrived home and exited the car, Pam got sick all over the newly-blossomed crocuses. At least the mess was outside.

As soon as we were inside the door, words poured out of Ash's mouth. "Mom, I'm sorry. I didn't mean to hurt Pam. She was drinking. And some creep was talking to her. I just wanted her to come home with me."

"Stop. Just stop." I did want to hear what happened, but I was exhausted. And the kids weren't in great shape either. "Ash, you need to get cleaned up and Pam has been drinking. We can't have a coherent discussion tonight. But I am angry enough to spit nails and we will have a discussion in the morning. Until then, you are both grounded for life or until I say otherwise. Pam, for drinking, and Ash, for hurting your sister. Now go to your rooms."

I heard footsteps on the stairs. "Hey, what's going on?" asked Phillip. He slowed down and then stopped at the sight of us at the bottom of the stairs. "Okay, I'm going back to bed." He turned around and went back up the steps.

"We are all going to bed," I said. "Ash, you are to stay in your room until your dad or I come to get you. Pam, the same goes for you, stay in your room until morning. We'll deal with this then."

"Mom, I'm not under the influence and I think we should talk about this now." Pam crossed her arms across her chest.

"Your vote will count when this becomes a democracy," I said. "Now, everybody is going to bed."

I followed Magda up the stairs. After we escorted Ash and Pam to their rooms, we got into bed. He fell asleep immediately. My mind kept going over the events of the night. It was now 4:00 a.m. and I was going over the points I wanted to make with the children in the morning. At 4:45 a.m., I was contemplating having to get a lawyer for Ash. I know Attorney Paoletti to be a good criminal defense attorney and he is known by the District Court judge. He was a bit aggressive with the restraining order last night, but that's not necessarily a bad thing. Hell, with the courthouse grapevine, everyone will probably know about Ash by the morning.

Ash, my quiet, retiring son. Why did he leave marks on his sister? Or was it all a misunderstanding? At 5:30 a.m., I fell asleep.

I woke up to the sun coming through my window and the smell of bacon cooking. It was 7:30 a.m. With a jolt, I remembered I promised to meet with Chloe in half an hour. I threw on some clothes, texted Chloe that I would be a few minutes late, and went downstairs.

"I'm calling you in sick today," said Magda. "Sit and eat." He slid a plate of eggs and toast in front of me.

"Can't." I picked up the toast and poured coffee into me stainless steel travel mug. "I promised Chloe I'd be there at eight. With coffee and pastry."

"We need to talk to the kids." Magda sat down. "Soon."

I stopped for a few moments. No noise outside the kitchen. The children were still asleep.

"From the looks of Pam last night, she won't be up for a few hours yet," I said. "I'll go see Chloe and be back by eleven so we can talk to the kids."

"Okay," said Magda. "I'll go into the factory for a few hours, get things straightened out."

I stood up. "No, you need to stay here with the kids. Make sure they're alright and they're still here at eleven."

Magda opened and closed his mouth. "I'll have Dave bring work over to the house. And make sure the kids stay grounded."

I left.

The parking lot at the Cushman Café was full when I pulled in. A free-standing building, with no drive-up window, the cook at the Cushman made a limited number of muffins, pastries, and other goodies each day. When they were gone, everyone had to wait until the next day to try again. I ordered three muffins, three chocolate croissants, and two coffees. That seemed like enough sugar and caffeine for whatever discussion needed to happen. I must have made the right choice, because Chloe smiled when she opened the bag.

"I set the table in the breakfast nook," said Chloe. "Let's eat back there."

I followed her down the hallway, past the living room, and into the kitchen. Two chairs and a small table sat in front of the bowed window. Though the window was covered with plants, not a dead leaf or a hanging cobweb was to be seen.

We sat down. Chloe took the pastries out of the bag and arranged them on a plate. She took the cardboard cups of coffee and poured the liquid into waiting mugs. "It used to drive Jenna crazy, but I can't stand to eat out of cardboard containers or paper bags." Chloe put the trash in a bin labelled recycle. "I'll miss having her complain about my habits."

I reached out and took Chloe's hand. "I miss her too. The courthouse won't be the same without her."

Chloe poured four sugars into her coffee. Maybe I was mistaken about the amount of sugar required for this conversation. We sat and ate in silence for a few minutes.

"I did want to talk to you," said Chloe. "About Jenna."

"She did seem out of sorts the past two weeks," I said. "She seldom misses work and never without calling." Only after I finished the sentence did I realize the tenses were wrong.

"She swore me to secrecy. Didn't want me to tell you what was going on." Chloe picked up crumbs with her finger and put them into her mouth. "It's hard for me to keep things from you."

"I knew something was wrong. I should have called."

Chloe made a motion with her hand, as if to brush away my

concerns. She then clasped her hands, took a deep breath and blurted out, "Jenna was pregnant."

I felt pushed back in my chair. Disappointment that they'd kept the news from me, and the pain of knowing the child would never be born. "I'm sorry you lost both of them."

Chloe stared out the window, at the birdfeeder hanging in the yard. "The jays drove all the other birds away this winter. I hope some of them come back now it's warmer. I'm thinking of putting up a hummingbird feeder. Jenna loved hummingbirds."

I took Chloe's hand again. "Why didn't you want me to know that Jenna was pregnant?"

Chloe looked directly at me. "Because we didn't know how you'd react. After the hard time you had with the twins."

"Because I had to stay in bed for three months?" The minute I asked the question I knew I was wrong.

"No." Chloe put her hands flat on the table. "Because you blamed the hard time you had with the twins on what happened with Heather."

I didn't say anything.

"How many people even know you had a child named Heather?" asked Chloe. "Me and Magda. Heather's father. And I told Jenna."

"My kids know," I said. "Not all the details, but they know I had a child I gave up for adoption." Now I stared out the window at the birdfeeder. "Why didn't you expect me to be glad for you?"

"We knew you'd be happy for us," Chloe picked up the dishes and brought them to the sink. "It's just, I know pregnancy and babies is a delicate subject and we wanted to tell you in private. Not have you hear a rumor around the courthouse."

"Thank you for telling me in private. Of course, now

everybody is going to know."

"Yeah, Jenna was so private, now everybody will know our business."

"Not to be indelicate," I said, "But who's the father?"

Chloe did the brushing motion with her hand again. "Technology was involved."

I grabbed a second chocolate croissant.

"What are you going to do now?" I asked.

"I'm the primary suspect in Jenna's death. The police have already been here." Chloe sat back down at the table. "Though I sort-of have an alibi, I am the surviving spouse."

"What is your sort-of alibi?"

"I spent most of the morning at school, in my office, working on a proposal for a before-school program. The police seem to think I could have snuck out, killed Jenna, gone back to the school, finished the proposal, and acted surprised when the police arrived."

"That requires some planning and fast driving." I couldn't keep the sarcasm out of my voice.

"Or I could have hired someone to do it." Chloe was good at sarcasm too.

"Let me know if I can do anything to help."

"Actually, you can." Chloe stared at the birdfeeder again. "You can ask questions in the courthouse, find out what's going on. Who had a problem with Jenna?"

"I meant, give you the name of a lawyer, help you make plans for the funeral. I'm not an investigator, I'm a judge."

"But you know what goes on at the courthouse. And, according to Jenna, there's a court officer who is plugged into everything there. He likes you."

"Cally," I said. "Yup, I go to him for all my information. But I'm still not sure I want to be part of the investigation."

"I'm dreading something else, too." Tears filled Chloe's eyes. "I have to go talk to Jenna's mother. Could you come with me?"

Chloe looked miserable. I agreed to go with her to see Jenna's mother and avoided a definite answer on asking questions around the courthouse.

After I left Chloe's house, I sat in the car for a few minutes. I didn't want to go see Jenna's mother. She never accepted Jenna and Chloe as a couple and her religion grated on my nerves. But I couldn't let Chloe do it alone. And I couldn't see what questions I could ask that the police hadn't already asked. I started the car and drove home to deal with the problem of my own children.

When I got home, Ash and Pam were in the kitchen with Magda. The kids were still in their pajamas. Ash was eating eggs and Pam picked at her dry toast.

"I don't eat bacon, or anything cooked with bacon," said Ash.

Pam stared at her brother. "He thinks he's a Muslim."

A full ten seconds of silence.

"I am a Muslim," said Ash.

"When did you decide this?" I asked.

"Last night, when he tried to spoil my fun." Pam continued to stare at her brother.

"Alright, "said Magda. "Let's talk about last night." He folded his hands on the table in front of him. "Let's start at the end. Did you lay your hands on your sister?"

Ash looked at the table as he spoke. "I tried to get her to come home with me. She was drunk."

"I was not drunk." Pam looked from Ash to me, and back to Ash. "I had a couple beers, but I wasn't drunk."

"You're fourteen." This from Magda, as if we all needed to be reminded. "And you vomited in the bushes."

I sat down at the table. "Okay, let's talk about what happened. Pam, you first."

Pam protested, "Why do I have to go first?" at the same time Ash said. "That's not fair."

"Okay, Ash, you go first." Magda interrupted them.

"I was driving home from the mosque," Ash started, then stopped. "I've been going to the mosque in Worcester. Islam is a religion of rules and rituals. Not like Christ dying for our sins and the eating his body and blood in church. That's cannibalism and necrophilia."

"I see the expensive private school education has improved your vocabulary, if not your outlook," said Magda.

"Don't stop him," I said. "Let him finish."

"I don't know whether I'm Muslim, but I might like to be. I like the people at the mosque, and they accept me. It is a problem giving up Dad's bacon though." His attempt at humor met with silence.

"So, I left late because I helped clean up after the singles event, and, coming down Oak Street, I see Pam walking down the grass in the middle. She tripped and almost lost her balance. I stopped. Thought I'd give her a ride."

"He stopped to hassle me and Simon," said Pam.

"Who's Simon?" This from Magda. He didn't know Simon was the older brother of her friend, Selena. Simon was old enough to buy alcohol, but I wasn't going to add that to the conversation.

"Lena's brother," she said. "We were hanging out together."

"After I stopped the car, they were very together." Ash played with the salt and pepper shaker, banging them together. "Pam was hanging all over him and he had his hands up her shirt."

I sensed, rather than felt, Magda stiffen beside me.

"Is that what happened?" I asked Pam

"Ash, the golden boy, the oldest, says it's true, so it must be."

"I'm asking you."

"Plead the Fifth," Pam said.

"That's what I saw," said Ash. "When I got closer, it was obvious they'd been drinking. They were holding each other up. So, I tried to get Pam in my car."

"Like a caveman," said Pam. "Me big brother, you get in car. I said no."

"She said Simon would drive her, but I didn't think that was a good idea. I threatened to call you guys, but she still wouldn't get in my car." Ash got up, took the teakettle off the stove, and started filling it with water.

"Simon would've given me a ride home." Pam crossed her arms over her body and leaned back in the chair.

"Hey, it isn't your time to talk yet," Ash said, as he placed the kettle back on the stove and turned on the burner.

"Thought you were finished," said Pam. "What with you being busy making tea. I already made coffee."

"I'm not finished," said Ash. "And I want some tea." He came back to the table.

"Anyway, she wouldn't get in my car." As he spoke, Ash took the dining room chair, turned it around, and sat in it backward. He knew I didn't like that but I didn't want to pick that fight. "I tried to pull her by the arm. Simon tried to stop me, there was some yelling and screaming, and somebody called the cops."

"He was so into yelling and pulling me that he didn't even hear the cops arrive." This from Pam, who looked more animated that she had all morning. "He was dragging me down the street. That's assault." Spoken like the daughter of a lawyer.

"So, they arrested me," said Ash. "And you know the rest."

"How did you get to the police station?" Magda's question was directed at Pam.

Pam leaned forward and put her elbows on the table. "Ash was making such a scene that they wouldn't let me leave with Simon. Said they'd arrest me for disorderly conduct if I didn't get in the car. And, because I'm a minor, they called the EMTs. They bandaged me up and left. So, my only choice was the police car."

"Simon was drunk. He couldn't drive you," said Ash.

"Simon was not drunk. You don't know what you're talking about." Pam got up from the table and stomped up the stairs.

"See, she's still being a bitch," said Ash.

"You will not talk about your sister that way." Magda's rules.

Pam stomped back into the room. We all looked up at her.

"And this is all because Ash thinks he's a Muslim and I'm being not modest, and he doesn't want anybody to drink or have any fun." With a flourish, Pam left the room for a second time.

"I don't want to discuss my religion," said Ash. He got up from the chair, went to the teapot, made his tea, and sat back down.

"Take your tea upstairs to your room and stay there until I tell you to come down," I said. "Your father and I need to talk."

"What are you going to talk about?"

"You, of course. We need to get you a lawyer and maybe a private investigator to interview the other people there that night. And we need to discuss your punishment here at home.

"Mom, it was just an argument."

"No, it was just an argument until the police arrived. Now it's a criminal matter. Go to your room and don't talk to anybody about what happened last night. No Facebook, no posts, no Snap-chat. Just tell everybody that your mother, the judge, will kill you if you talk. Give me your phone. Clear?"

"Clear." Ash placed his phone on the table, took his tea, and left.

I sat and stared at Magda. "What do we do now?"

"Get him a lawyer, I guess. Do you know anybody?" Magda got up and started clearing the table. I guess he had to be upset, he was doing housework. Not good, concentrate on the problem.

"Gerard Paoletti. He's probably the best. And I just met his son in the park the other day, so he has some experience dealing with teenagers. He's leaving his practice in juvenile court to do personal injury law, but he has contacts in the District Court. It may do it as a personal favor to me."

"You didn't tell me you went to the park. Or that you met anyone." Magda turned around to look at me.

"A lot has been going on. It was just a casual meeting."

Magda stared out the window. "What about Pamela?"

"She may need a lawyer too. She's fourteen years old and drinking." I went to stand by Magda. "Or maybe a counselor. Fourteen is awfully young to develop such bad habits."

"How can you be so calm?" asked Magda. "I'll call Paoletti, make an appointment. You go talk to Pam. Get her to stop drinking and hanging out with guys older than she is."

"I don't know if I can do that," I said. "I'll be happy if she acknowledges she did a dumb thing and promises not to do it again."

"Why aren't you freaking out?" Magda's voice got noticeably louder. "She's fourteen, she's drinking alcohol. Alcohol supplied, most likely, by this Simon character. God only knows what he was expecting in return for buying it."

I'd had the same thought, but it sounded much more ominous when Magda laid it out that way. "I am freaking out, on the inside. I just don't think yelling at Pam will do a lot of good."

"I thought grounding her for life was a nice touch."

I laughed at Magda's weak attempt at humor.

"I'll make the call; you talk to Pam." Magda went into the den.

I took my time going up the stairs. How do you tell a four-teen-year-old girl not to do something without making it seem glamourous and forbidden? And Pam was my impulsive child. Phillip or Ash would think things over, even if after the fact. Pam was a good girl, a great student, she could figure this out.

I knocked on her door. "Can I come in?"

"You're going to anyway." She opened the door.

Good, at least I didn't have to stand out in the hall and yell at her through the door. Though I was prepared to do it and hope it embarrassed her enough that she would let me in.

She stepped back from the door and sat on her bed. I went into the room and sat on the wooden chair at her desk.

"I know it was a dumb thing to do," Pam said.

"Which thing?" I was feeling tired and bitchy. "The staying out after curfew or the drinking or hanging out with a boy to get alcohol or drinking or arguing with your brother?"

"I'm not sorry about arguing with Ash. He was being an asshole."

"That may be true, and he is dealing with the consequences of his actions," I said. "Let's talk about what you did."

"It's not like you didn't drink and have a boyfriend when you were my age."

"This isn't about me, it's about you. And I was nineteen years old, you are fourteen. You are way too young to be making decisions that may affect your whole life."

Pam fell back on her bed, sighing as she fell. "It's not like we were having sex."

Sex at fourteen. I'm glad that's not an issue. But I made a note to call my gynecologist and make an appointment for Pam. Better to be prepared.

"But you were drinking," I said. "And I'm not so sure Simon wasn't thinking about sex."

"Of course, Simon was thinking about sex. Guys are always thinking about sex and how to get it and who will give it to them."

I was in my twenties before I figured that out. Maybe I was a slow learner.

"Besides, that's why I stayed with Phillip." She sat up again. "With him there, I figured I was safe. Then he wimped out and went home."

"So, it's Philip's fault because he wanted to be home for curfew?"

"It was like 10:04. He could've waited for me."

"Or you could have come home for your curfew," I said. "Anyway, you are grounded for a month. You can go to school, go to ballet, and go to softball. Other than that, you are at home or with your father or me."

"Ma, it's the end of school. I won't see some of my friends all summer. I need to see them now."

"No, you don't. If you must see someone, your father or I will go with you."

"Yeah, like the two of you are around so much."

My mother is an English professor. I am good at subtext, the meaning under the words. "If I can't trust you to come home and stay home, I can hire someone to watch you and make sure you stay home. Or you can go to the factory and work with your father after school. I'm sure he can give you a job filing in the office or making copies or something."

"Nothing's on paper these days. Dad computerized everything years ago."

I stood up. "That is not the point. Do I have your word that you will come directly home after school? If not, I will make other arrangements."

"No, I'll come home after school."

"And no friends over to visit. You are grounded."

Her wail followed me down the stairs.

Magda stood at the bottom of the stairs. "I see it went well," he said. "Or rather, I hear it."

"I grounded her for a month. If she doesn't come home directly from school, I told her she would have to go to the factory and hang out with you."

"You mean work?" He laughed. "A fate worse than death." He started up the stairs. "On a different topic, I called Attorney Paoletti and he said he could see us this afternoon. He's working at home, but he'll see us as a favor to you. I'm going to get Ash."

Paoletti's house sat back from the road. We drove up the white, crushed stone driveway for several minutes. Huge trees hung over the drive, just beginning to green. The driveway ended in a round-about and a small parking area. The house was an old Federalist mansion with stone steps.

"Nice set-up," said Ash. "Can you guys afford him?"

"We can afford him because he is getting out of the local court work. He had a huge recovery on a personal injury matter and he's decided to concentrate in that area." I'd gathered this information from the courthouse gossip. And because Jenna had been planning his going-away party. "You may be his last criminal case."

"Lucky me."

We got out of the car and Magda rang the doorbell. It was answered immediately by a woman in a pencil skirt and pearls.

"You must be Judge Hartwell," she said. "I'm Sylvia, Gerard's wife."

She stepped back and let us enter the home. Like many Federalist houses, the entryway was narrow, with stairs going up the right side. The stairs were oak and mahogany.

"My home office is a mess," Paoletti said, as he entered the room. "I'm in the middle of trial prep for a motor vehicle case and there is paper everywhere. We can meet in the solarium."

The solarium was a huge glass structure added on to the house. It overlooked a pond and was overflowing with vegetation. Mrs. Paoletti followed us to the solarium.

"Sylvia and I love plants." Paoletti motioned us to upholstered chairs set by the middle window. "We try to have blooms around us all year long."

"I was admiring the trees when we came up the driveway," I said.

"Thank you, those trees are a special treat. Of course, the gardeners keep the outside," Paoletti explained, "but Sylvia and I do all the work in here ourselves."

We all settled in and Paoletti took some basic information, including who to bill for this representation. I brought up the potential conflict of interest issue but Paoletti had it sorted out. His personal injury practice was thriving and he wanted to discontinue his juvenile court practice. This case gave him reason to withdraw from all his juvenile court cases, so he would not appear in front of me again. I knew that, of course, but wanted it settled before the representation began.

Paoletti asked Magda and me to leave the room.

"Why do we have to leave the room?" asked Magda. "We're his parents."

Magda knew damn well why we needed to leave; he'd been married to a lawyer for twenty years. But Paoletti was patient and explained it to him.

"Everything that Ashroff tells me is confidential," he said. "I can't discuss what we say with anyone else and we can be candid about our trial strategy. If either of you are in the room, and Ash makes an incriminating statement," Paoletti stopped talking when Magda leaned forward, "or even an ambiguous statement that contradicts something he says in court, the prosecution can call you as a witness. You and Abbi are not my clients, so there is no privilege. You could end up testifying against your own son."

"It's even more important because Ash is eighteen years old." Paoletti folded his hands on the desk and continued. "He's not entitled to have a parent present; he's deemed capable of making his own decisions. So, even if you discuss this at home, and then tell someone else what he said, you could be called to testify. So, you need to leave."

Magda stayed in his seat. "Why isn't your wife leaving the room?" He gestured toward Sylvia Paoletti, standing silently by the window.

"My wife is an attorney also," Paoletti said.

I couldn't keep the surprise from my face. I'd practiced law for almost twenty years, had appeared in front of dozens of judges, and had never heard of Sylvia Paoletti as an attorney.

"I don't appear in court," she said, from the back of the room.

"I do legal research, some writing, and I run the office. But I am a licensed attorney."

Magda got up slowly and left with me.

It was torture, sitting in the hallway, waiting for Ash to appear again. Maybe worse than sitting in the police station. At the police station, I knew that, eventually, someone would come out and explain things to us. Ash may never tell us what he and Paoletti discussed. I'm sure Paoletti was impressing upon him the importance of not discussing the case with anyone.

As I had nothing else to do, I did an internet search on Sylvia Paoletti, both a general search and a search of legal databases. She was listed as Sylvia Flannery Paoletti and she had been a lawyer longer that I had. Assuming Flannery was her birth name, I checked her background. She attended University of Pennsylvania Law School and was the editor of the Law Review there. She spent a few years at the public defender's office and then went to work for her husband's law firm. His firm was listed as her business address, her bar dues were current, and she had no history of bar discipline.

As the minutes dragged on, I did a search on Gerard Paoletti. He also went to the University of Pennsylvania Law School, but didn't seem to make much of an impression there. No law review, no competitions or prizes. He opened his own office right out of law school, had moved its location twice, and was disciplined eight years ago, and again five years ago, both for neglecting a client matter. He was president of the local bar association and active in the Chamber of Commerce and the Rotary. His career took off when he started writing articles for several legal publications about five years ago. His legal writing ability seemed to have improved dramatically from law school.

It seemed like hours, but Ash appeared about fifty minutes later. Paoletti followed him into the corridor.

"I've told him not to discuss the case with anyone but me," said Paoletti. He looked at Magda. "And that includes his parents. We're finished for today. But I'll need to see him again before the arraignment. They'll send you notice in the mail. Please let me know as soon as you are notified of the date. I can't enter an appearance until the case is filed, so I may not be notified of the first date."

I had a list of things I wanted to say to Ash, but I forced myself to remain silent on the ride home.

FRIDAY

THE ATMOSPHERE AT THE COURTHOUSE WAS TENSE AND jumpy. The whole building, not just the people in it. Court officers wore black bands on their badges. The police were going through Jenna's tiny office. The First Justice was not in the building; she was meeting with the police chief who wanted access to juvenile court files. The files were confidential and impounded and the First Justice was adamant that they would not be released. I had no idea how that confrontation would end.

I nodded to the few people I met on my way to the office, logged in on my computer, and entered a notice that I would be leaving early that day to accompany Chloe to the funeral home. My docket was crowded but since it was a motion day, I hoped most of the cases could be disposed of quickly. Of course, because it was Friday, the possibility of an emergency filing was high. No logical reason, just more cases were filed at the end of the week.

Cally knocked on the door my office. Usually he just stuck his head in, but today he waited for me to say "come in."

He stood at attention just inside the door. "Just came to check with you about your plans for today."

"Sit down." I gestured toward the chair across from my desk. "Things seem tense around here today."

"Everybody is sorry about Jenna and jumpy about someone being murdered in the courthouse." He adjusted himself in the chair and looked at me. "I know the police talked to you. I just wanted you to know that I told them that you and Jenna were talking and gesturing in the garage. That you stepped in front of Jenna when she tried to leave and that she pushed you out of the way and left."

"You described it as an argument."

"I think I said a disagreement," said Cally. "I didn't know whether you were arguing, I couldn't hear the words." He looked around the room. "I didn't mean to get you into trouble. I don't believe that you would hurt Jenna."

"But you told the police about it." I leaned back in my chair.

"You know I had to. You were in the public garage. If someone else had talked about it, and I was there and said nothing, it would look bad."

He did have a point. Not that it made my discussion with the police any more pleasant.

"The courthouse is buzzing with theories about Jenna's death," said Cally. "And the police are asking me endless questions about security."

I recognized his statement for the peace offering it was. As a judge, I was isolated in my office or in the courtroom most of the day. There were strict rules about socializing with attorneys and I was not allowed to talk to jurors. Cally was my eyes and ears about what was going on in the courthouse corridors.

"What are they saying?" I was asking to ascertain morale, not to gossip. Or that's what I told myself.

"There's no shortage of theories or suspects." I saw Cally relax for the first time since he came into the room. "Dissatisfied defendant, someone she slighted without knowing it, there's even a theory she got into it with the cafeteria owner and he stabbed her with his knife."

"I thought Jenna was shot, not stabbed."

"That's true," Cally said, "but it doesn't stop the talk. Also, there's a rumor that she was pregnant and then there's a whole love triangle thing."

It was going to be public anyway, in the near future. "Jenna was pregnant." I waited a few moments. "You don't seem surprised."

"I'm not." Cally spoke softly, like he wanted to keep the admission a secret. "I'm the father of three, I know the symptoms. She was out of work and often in the ladies' room in the morning. I never asked her about it, though." He looked out the window, at the weak sun. "How do you know?"

"I went to see Chloe last night. Her reasons for not telling me seemed less than compelling, but maybe they were just stressed."

"Everybody's stressed," said Cally. "And they're talking about implementing new security procedures. I keep telling them it won't work unless they hire more people to check on all the ways in and out of this building."

I stood up. "Is there anything you need from me?"

"Don't think so." Cally stood up also. "Let's get started on the day."

The morning was a blur of motions, conferences, and an emergency filing, as predicted. I finished at about two and texted Chloe to let her know I was on the way. She offered to meet me at the funeral home, but I didn't think she should drive today.

Chloe came out of her house, put her purse on the floor of my car, and said, "I can't believe we're going to do this."

We left the residential area and headed toward the town center.

"When do you think they'll release her body?" asked Chloe.

"I don't know. When the medical examiner is finished with it, I guess."

"Jenna wanted to be cremated. She told me that." Chloe picked her purse up and pulled out a packet of Kleenex. "Should I cremate her?"

I didn't know what to say.

"Or should I have her body preserved, in case they need more evidence later?" Chloe continued on as if talking to herself. "In the forensic shows, they can dig up the body if new evidence is found. They can't do that if she's ashes."

"Chloe, you don't have to make these decisions now. We don't have to go now. We can wait, if you want to."

"No, we can't." Chloe stared out the window. "I want to do a celebration of her life, not a wake. That way I can just schedule it and won't have to wait for the medical examiner."

I pulled up in front of the funeral home. We were greeted by a large man wearing a blue blazer and no tie. He introduced himself as Mr. Knight, second generation of the Baker-Knight funeral home.

Much of what came next was a blur. I remember the funeral director asking Chloe to make endless decisions. About prayer cards and pictures to display and hymns. Endless details to consider. Chloe asked Mr. Knight about a "celebration of life." I was hungry and tired and cranky. It seemed bizarre to have a celebration of life in a funeral home.

"We will need bowls for candies," Chloe said.

The funeral director looked at me.

Chloe smiled. "Peppermint candies," she said.

"Yes. In big bowls." I held my hands about eight inches apart, to show the size of the bowl. "Jenna's office and house always had peppermint candies in big bowls. She offered them to everyone who came in."

Chloe seemed to be taking this better than I was. She cried more, but the activity and the decisions seemed to energize her and give her a reason to talk about Jenna. Her thoughts seemed to run along lines similar to mine.

"Maybe I don't want Jenna's farewell to be from a funeral home," said Chloe. "I want a party, maybe at the Academy of Music. Then we can have candy, and music, and lots of pictures of Jenna."

"The Academy of Music?" Mr. Knight's voice rose an octave.

"It's a little theatre downtown," said Chloe. Her enthusiasm rose as she spoke. "We can all sit around and talk about Jenna, rather than staring at a casket or an urn." Chloe pulled out her phone and pressed buttons. "Shirl, it's Chloe…Yes, I'm going to miss her…I want to have Jenna's celebration of life at the Academy." A few more minutes and the celebration was scheduled for Wednesday night from six to nine.

"You won't need the services of the funeral parlor?" Mr. Knight was a little slow catching on.

"I'll have the body delivered here when the medical examiner is finished with it. By then, I'll make a decision what to do next." Chloe's voice had a different quality. She wasn't happy, but she was doing something for Jenna.

We left the funeral home with promotional materials for invitations and picture displays. It was easier to accept them than to argue with Mr. Knight. I was exhausted by the time I finished.

I don't remember much going home or what I did there. I went to bed early and slept through the night.

SATURDAY

MY FACE WAS SLICK WITH ANTI-AGING SERUM WHEN THE phone rang on Saturday morning. From the bathroom, I heard Magda scramble for the phone and mumble something that sounded like words.

"Abbi," he called. "It's for you."

I came out of the bathroom. "Who is it?"

"Dale." Magda glared at me. "What does he want now?"

He handed me the phone.

Dale started in without saying hello. "Abbi, something's happened to your mother."

I couldn't make words.

"Abbi," Dale's voice got lower. "I'm sorry to tell you this way."

My eyes darted randomly around the bedroom. My bed, my clothing, my husband, all the familiar everyday things. My mind returned to the phone and Dale telling me the not-so-normal.

I picked up the "South Will Rise" paperweight that was my father's, so many years ago. "What happened?"

"She was out walking this morning. She was hit by a car. She's at Cheshire Medical Center. They say she has a broken femur. She's in surgery."

"That doesn't make any sense. My mother wouldn't be out

walking alone."

"I know." Dale stopped talking for a moment. "It was a hit and run. A deserted road, she had on a reflective vest, and somebody hit her and drove away."

"What condition is she in?"

"She's in the operating room. We'll know more in a few hours."

I stared out the window. "She was wearing her reflective vest? She planned to go out walking in the morning?"

"I can't figure it out either," said Dale. "I left for the gym about seven and she was having breakfast. We meet every Saturday at ten-thirty to talk about and edit my work. I finished at the gym, went to the bakery and the gas station, and arrived back a little after ten-thirty. She had identification on her, because the police arrived at the house almost immediately after I did."

"I'll be there in about an hour." I ended the call.

Magda looked at me.

"My mother had an accident. I need to go see her today."

Magda put his arms around me. "What can I do?"

"Deal with the kids until I get back."

"When will that be?"

"I don't know." I stepped away from him and got my suitcase out of the closet. "It depends on what happens after she gets out of surgery." I explained what Dale told me a few minutes ago. "I'm going to pack a suitcase, to be ready if I need to stay there."

"So, you'll be spending time with Dale?"

"It's hard to avoid," I said. "He lives with her."

Magda came over and put his arms around me again. "I don't like you being with him."

"Yeah, we have history." I wasn't getting into this now. Twenty years ago, Dale and I thought we were in love. I had a child that

I gave up for adoption. I'm not going to think about that now or I'll burst into tears.

"Why did your mother decide to hire him as her caretaker, of all the people in the world?"

"My mother has known Dale for thirty years. After he wrote his first few books, he decided to get his MFA at Keene State. My mother was his mentor, he rented a room from her about six months ago. He takes care of her and she edits his work." That was the shortened version of their history.

"I know that," said Magda. "I just don't like it." He went into the bathroom.

I'm awful at packing. I shuffled through the clothes in my closet, guessed at what I needed, and stuffed them into the suitcase. Second guessing, I took another look, saw more things I might need, and tried to jam them in as well. The suitcase wouldn't close, so I had to make decisions about what to keep and what to leave behind. I'm not good at leaving behind. After my last trip, my suitcase came off the baggage carousel with the zipper busted open and clothes spilling out.

How long would I be staying with my mother in New Hampshire? I had no idea but thought I should take clothing for at least a few days. It was only about an hour from Meredith to Keene, so I could come back for more things or have someone bring them to me.

I was hot and sweaty and frustrated and feeling overwhelmed. Magda walked back into the bedroom.

"Are you really going to do this?" he asked.

"No, I thought I'd practice my packing."

"You don't have to get pissy."

"I 'm not pissy. I'm worried about my mother and I want a

little support from my family." I threw more pairs of underwear into the suitcase.

Magda fingered an aqua pair with bows on them. "Mighty fancy underwear for a trip to your mother's house."

Now we were going to fight about my underwear. "I need clean underwear. All my white cotton is in the wash." Not exactly true, but close enough.

"We have problems when you aren't here. Not even the washing gets done."

"Hire the housekeeper back while I'm gone." I threw in a white shirt and two pairs of black slacks. Nothing sexy about those.

"Here, let me get that." Magda closed the suitcase, picked it up, and went downstairs.

I finished getting dressed and joined him in the kitchen. He and Ash sat at the table.

"How's Gramma doing?" asked Ash.

"She's in surgery. I'll know more when I get there. But it sounds serious."

"Do you want me to go with you?" This offer came from Ash, not Magda.

"No," I said. "I don't know what's going on. I'll let you know after I see Gramma."

Ash nodded.

"Where are Pam and Phillip?" I asked.

"They're still asleep." Ash seemed to be taking the conversational burden. "Or, Phillip was and I didn't hear anything from Pam's room."

"Should I wait until they're awake to tell them about Gramma?" I asked. "Or, maybe, wake them up?"

"I put your suitcase in the car," said Magda. "Why don't you just leave and I'll let them know what's going on? It's not like you can't call, or text, or Skype, or Facetime, or send a letter."

"Okay, I get the message." I kissed both of them and left.

When I reached Keene, I was hot and angry. Not a specific, focused anger, with a definite target. Just a low hanging, dark, seething anger at traffic, the police, my kids, security, my husband, and Jenna, for dying. And who the hell expected it to be seventy-five degrees in New Hampshire in April? I'd worn my long-sleeve shirt.

I don't remember the ride. Maybe it was a defense mechanism. The car pulled up at my mother's house; it's a good thing it knew the way.

When my great-grandfather bought the cottage in the 1930s, it was a workman's home. Over the years, on the edge of the city, it was now prime real estate. My mother rattled around in it alone.

I carried the luggage up the front steps and knocked on the door. Several minutes passed before I realized that my mother was at the hospital and would not answer. I pushed the front door. It wasn't locked. Dumped my bags on the floor.

As I walked through the living room, past the massive stone fireplace, it looked as though my mother had just finished breakfast. The dishes were on the table, with the newspaper neatly folded in half for easier reading. I made myself a cup of tea and tripped over the cat's dishes. I hoped the cat hadn't escaped out the open front door. Add finding the cat to my to-do list.

I texted Dale: *Just arrived at my mother's house. Are you at the hospital?*

My phone rang a few minutes later. Dale always preferred to call rather than text.

"I'm at the hospital," he said. "Your mother is still in surgery.

I can stay another hour or so, but I'm supposed to do a workshop this afternoon at the university. I can cancel it, if you need me to."

"I probably should have gone to the hospital first, but I couldn't convince myself that my mother would not be home to greet me and make tea," I said. "Let me look around the house, let me see if I can find her insurance information. I have her health care proxy with me."

"Her Medicare card was in her wallet, but I guess it wouldn't hurt to see if she has any other insurance."

"Don't cancel your afternoon workshop. I'll be at the hospital within the hour."

"See you then." Dale ended the call.

My mobile phone rang again. The readout on the phone said, "Commonwealth of Massachusetts." I didn't want to deal with work now, especially an overachieving person who was working on Saturday. I dropped the phone and it slid under a shelf in the kitchen. As I knelt on the floor to retrieve the phone, the floor felt greasy. Maybe my mother was sick even before the recent mishap. The floor had been mopped every week, without fail, for the last twenty years.

I reached under the bottom shelf, just inches from the floor. If my mother was not cleaning regularly, I didn't even want to think about what was under there. The ends of my fingers found the phone. My nose was pressed up against a cedar box on the bottom shelf. My mother's keepsake box. When I was younger, I would go through it on rainy days. A local furniture store gave the boxes to every girl in my mother's high school graduating class. A miniature hope chest; it encouraged the girls to return to purchase a full size one to prepare for their wedding. Did brides even have hope chests anymore? I am certain no stores were giving out the boxes anymore.

After some maneuvering, I retrieved the phone. As I had nothing else to do, I picked up the box and sat down at the dining room table. My mother might need insurance cards and other information for the hospital. For the last forty years, all that information had been kept in this box, though the key was missing and had been since I was a toddler. I lifted the cover.

Inside were old insurance policies on the house and papers on the last car my father had owned when he died five years ago. My mother's birth and wedding certificates and my birth and wedding certificates. Somehow, my mother acquired birth certificates on my children. No medical information.

At the bottom of the box lay a red book with smiley faces and peace signs stuck to the outside. I opened the cover and found, in my twenty-one-year old penmanship, the words "Abbi's Diary." I flipped through the pages and out fell a paper plane ticket, for an Air Egypt flight from Aswan to Cairo and then a ticket for the Cairo Tower. I'd only been to Egypt once, when I met Magda. Wonder why my mother saved my diary for over twenty years. I set it aside to deal with later.

Then I remembered that a phone call had started my search under the shelves. Though I didn't recognize the number, the voicemail was from Niagara Fontaine, an attorney for the Department of Children and Families. She said she had a personal matter to discuss with me. I don't usually discuss personal matters with attorneys, but she said it was important.

She picked up on the first ring. "Judge Hartwell, thanks for calling me back," she said. "This is a bit awkward for me, but I need your help."

"You said you wanted to discuss a personal matter," I picked up the red diary and turned it over. "I can't have discussions with you about any cases, without all the attorneys involved being present."

"I know that," she said. "This isn't an *ex parte* communication. I want to talk to you about my brother."

"Your brother?" I'd never heard Attorney Fontaine discuss any of her siblings.

"Yes, I have a biological brother. I haven't seen him in years. We've been emailing each other for the last few months and we have decided it's time to meet in person. You met him in the park yesterday."

"Richard Paoletti? He's your brother?" Now I was totally confused.

"Yes, he was adopted and I went into the child welfare system. We recently learned about each other and want to meet." This sentence came out in one long breath, as if Niagara needed to complete the sentence before she breathed.

I'd given a child up for adoption over twenty years ago. What if I learned that she had been living in the same neighborhood all this time? I didn't want to think about that.

"Why are you calling me?" I asked.

"Well, Richard and I want to meet for the first time with a neutral person present. Most of the people I know are connected with the Department or the court. I was wondering whether you could suggest an appropriate mediator." Niagara stopped to breath.

I thought about meeting my now twenty-one-year-old daughter. I think I'd want to be alone with her, just to study her. Maybe not. How well had Niagara and her brother thought this out?

"Richard and I have been communicating by email," Niagara

continued. "We've agreed to meet at a local restaurant or public place. I just want you to suggest someone who will be good as a mediator. I'm willing to pay them."

It sounded like something I could do. "Let me think about it and ask some people. I'll get back to you."

"Thanks," said Niagara. "I appreciate anything you can do."

I was ready to see my mother. Dale said she was in surgery, but I wanted to be there when she woke up.

The Cheshire Medical Center was a brick building on Court Street in Keene. Downtown was much as I remembered it. No skyscrapers, no buildings over three stories high.

I walked into the lobby. Chrome and plastic chairs and a receptionist behind a desk. Without thought to security; no glass separated her from the public.

I approached the woman behind the glass; she was filing her nails. "I'm looking for Mrs. Donnelly, please."

I noticed a movement off to the right. Moved aside and it moved with me.

"Mrs. Hartwell?"

I turned to face the heavy-set man. "It's Judge Hartwell."

He flashed a badge at me. "Judge Hartwell, I need to talk to you." I saw the tattoo of a snake around his wrist. The ouroboros, the ancient snake eating its own tail. My liberal arts education was good for something.

"I'm here to see my mother, who is ill. Can this wait?" I attempted to go around him.

"No, it can't." He moved to block my way. "It will only take a few minutes."

I hesitated.

"It's about your clerk, Jenna Jay."

In my efforts to get to my mother, I had pushed poor Jenna to the back of my mind. She was dead. My mother was in surgery. Neither needed my immediate attention. But the officer did not seem inclined to go away.

"What do you want?"

"I need to get your statement. The Massachusetts authorities want it soon."

"I already gave my statement."

"I have some additional questions."

I asked the receptionist to let me know when my mother came out of surgery. The large man led me to a conference room off the main lobby. More steel and plastic chairs and industrial green walls. Someone had tried to soften the place by hanging seascapes on the wall. Whaling ships and custom houses that no longer existed in New England. The clock said it was after three. I hadn't thought to ask when Dale's workshop began.

The officer looked around the room. "You've been told about the circumstances of Ms. Jay's death?"

I stared at him. "Yes, I think so."

He laid a file on the table. Where did that come from? I hadn't noticed it earlier.

"I don't have much." He turned the few pages in the file. "Ms. Jay was found shot in the parking garage under the court-house. Did you see anyone suspicious when you came into the courthouse?"

"No. I was surprised when the court officers came to lock down my courtroom. I didn't see Jenna that morning."

He closed the file. "Nobody's come forward to say they saw her. What time does Ms. Jay generally get to work?"

"About 7:30 or 8:00 a.m. She likes to get in early and get

things organized for the day."

The officer opened the file again. "She called a Dennis Raymond, from her cell phone, at 7:53 a.m. Do you know who he is?"

"Don't know anyone by that name." I pushed down the cuffs of my long-sleeve shirt. It was even warmer in the tiny room that it was outside. "Who is he?"

"We're working on that."

I said nothing.

"Course we're waiting for the medical examiner to determine the time of death," he added. "Until then, I have some questions."

"What do you want to know?"

"When was the last time you saw Ms. Jay?"

It took me a minute to remember. So much had happened since then. "We talked, in the courthouse, the afternoon before she died. This was in my previous statement."

"We just need to check."

"What did you say your name was?" It wasn't like me to forget names and identifying information.

"I didn't say. But it's Barry Stowell."

Something wasn't right. No police officer introduced himself by his full name. At least none that I had ever met.

"Was Gerard Paoletti there?" asked Mr. Stowell.

I stared at Stowell. Where had that query come from? "I don't know."

"Are you positive?"

This was going beyond weird. "What police department did you say you were with?"

"I didn't say I was a police officer," said Barry Stowell. "That's just what you assumed."

He was right. I didn't even ask for identification. "Then who the hell are you?"

"Barry Stowell." He pulled a wallet from his pocket and flipped it open. There lay the badge he'd shown me earlier. "I'm a private investigator."

"Who do you work for, Mr. Stowell?" Not that I expected an honest answer.

"I can't tell you," he said. "But it's someone who is very interested in Ms. Jay and the baby that she was carrying." He put the wallet back into his coat pocket. "Where did you and Ms. Jay have your conversation?"

"I'm done answering questions." I stood up.

"Were you in the judge's lobby? Are you sure nobody ever enters the judge's lobby without permission?"

People let others into the lobby all the time. Clerks, attorneys, anybody that was recognized. Sometimes anybody in a suit. I remembered when I was first a judge, trying to open doors without my access card and setting off alarms. If the court officers were busy, it took several minutes before anyone came to investigate. Not that I was going to share any more information with Mr. Stowell.

"Any access cards missing?" he asked.

"I've finished talking about this." I turned to leave the room.

Stowell opened the door for me. "I hope your mother's doing okay." He left.

I went back to the receptionist, who directed me to the surgery waiting area. Dale was in the back of the room, reading a book. As I got closer, I saw his name on the cover.

"Reading your own work?" I asked.

He looked up. "The workshop is on setting and atmosphere

in my books. Thought I'd do some last-minute cramming." He closed the book. "No further information on your mother since I talked to you. I'll be leaving now. Don't know how long the students will want to talk to me after the workshop, so I can't say when I'll be back at the house." He stood up. "Text me if you need me. I'll check it a few times during the evening." He left.

I called Magda. "Magda, something just happened and it's freaking me out."

"Something with your mother? Is she all right? Are you all right?"

"No, nothing about my mother."

"Have you talked to her?" Something crashed on the other end of the phone.

"No, I'm waiting for her to get out of surgery," I said. "What was that sound?"

"Ash and Pam are having another discussion. I think she's making a dramatic point. As you said, nothing unusual, given the participants. What's bothering you?"

"A man came up to me in the hospital with questions about the murder of Jenna."

"You knew the police would be talking to you." I heard Magda open the refrigerator.

"He wasn't the police. He was a private investigator and I'm in another state. He knew Jenna was pregnant."

"Yeah, it was in the paper this morning. Fourth or fifth paragraph." Magda was the only person I knew that read the local paper, cover to cover. "Guess it's not private anymore."

"But he tried to pass himself off as a police officer. I should've known better, but I answered his questions."

"Isn't impersonating a police officer a crime? Even in New

Hampshire?"

"Yeah," I agreed. "What am I going to tell the cops? This man with an interesting tattoo came up to me and I assumed he was a cop and answered his questions?"

"Doesn't sound like much of a crime, if you put it that way," Magda said. "What's this about an interesting tattoo?"

"Around his wrist, a tattoo of a snake eating its tail. It's an ancient symbol of eternal life, called an ouroboros," I said. "Maybe I'm making too much of this. Is everything else working out?"

Magda assured me that the house was still standing and the children hadn't done anything other than the usual chaos. I didn't press him for details.

"How is you mother doing?" I could hear Magda chopping something.

"She came through the surgery. I just got into the recovery room. I'd like to be here when she wakes up. I'll probably stay the night and call you tomorrow to let you know how it's looking."

"We'll be here. Take care of yourself and your mother."

I tapped off the phone. A hospital volunteer came to tell me that my mother was in the recovery room. I went to see her. She was gray. Gray hair, gray skin, even the sheets looked gray. I sat down beside the bed.

A nurse bustled over to check the heart monitor and the IV drip.

"Hello, I'm Loretta Jones. I'm the nurse caring for Mrs. Donnelly. Are you her daughter?"

I stood up. "Yes. Abbi Hartwell." We shook hands.

"Do you have any questions about your mother?

I started with the obvious. "When will she wake up?"

"The surgery went well, though she'll still need many weeks

of rehabilitation. The anesthesia should wear off in about a half hour, but she may be confused for a short while."

"How bad are her injuries? Why was she walking along the road so early in the morning?"

The nurse went to the computer monitor next to the bed. "There's nothing here about the circumstances that got her to the hospital. Just that she arrived with a broken femur, some bruised ribs, and several hematomas on her legs. The bruises and the ribs will heal. The femur has been repaired, but it will be several weeks, at least, before she can walk on it."

"Will you do the rehab here?"

"No, she'll probably be sent to an acute orthopedic rehab. The social worker will be here on Monday and can talk to you about how that will work." The nurse pushed some more buttons on her monitor. "We have a copy of her health care proxy, appointing you to make decisions if she can't. We're concerned about her heart. She had a minor stroke a few months ago, and she refused to go on warfarin or any other blood thinner. We need to address that problem. It is highly recommended that she take blood thinners to reduce her risk of future strokes."

"She did the health care proxy about ten years ago. I have a paper copy here." I patted my purse. "And she'd been refusing to take blood thinners most of that time."

The nurse smile and bustled away. I suddenly realized how tired I was.

My mother was slumped down in the bed. I adjusted the pillows and pulled her back into the center. Her eyes popped open.

"Thank you, dear," she said. "Are you here to get me ready for surgery?"

"No, Ma, I'm your daughter Abbi."

"Abbi?" She looked around the room. "My daughter is Amythyst Basil. Isn't that a lovely name?"

"Yes, it is a lovely name." I brought a chair near her bed and sat down. "But I'm a judge now and I go by A.B. or Abbi."

"Oh, Abbi. Oh, yes, you're the mother of Ashroff, Pam, and Phillip. How foolish of me." She stared out the window.

"You had your surgery this morning," I said. "You're in the recovery room"

"Is that why my leg hurts?" She tried to push aside the covers.

I took her hands in mine. "Ma, don't do that. You need to heal. Just lie back and relax."

An intercom announced the end of visiting hours. Nurse Jones came back in and made arrangements for my mother to be moved to the critical care unit. This involved a ride on the gurney through the hospital corridors and a transfer to a hospital bed. At last, it was just my mother and me.

"How are you doing?" I tucked the blankets around my mother.

"Okay." My mother looked around the room. "Am I in the hospital?"

"Yes, ma. You had surgery today."

"Did I? I don't remember anything after breakfast."

"You don't remember walking on the road? Getting hit?"

"I don't think so." My mother shook her head. "I'm tired. I'm going to sleep now."

I left.

I stopped at the drive-through at McDonald's for dinner. I'd see if I could salvage breakfast at my mother's house.

When I got back to my mother's house, it seemed even larger

and more deserted than when I left. My mother's breakfast dishes were still on the table. I picked them up and washed them.

Dale lived in two rooms on the second floor. I didn't hear him and I hadn't seen his car in the driveway. The students must be keeping him occupied.

When I went to wipe off the table, I saw the wooden box and my diary that I had removed earlier. I'd hauled that diary all over Europe and Africa during the year between college and law school. It looked it; there were unidentifiable stains on the cover and some pages were yellow and curled. That was a tough year. Maybe that's why my mother saved it.

I opened the cover and began reading:

Today we arrived in Egypt. I met Peta at the hostel in Denmark; she comes from one of the other Nordic countries and is taking a tour of the world. She's older than me, had been working a few years, quit her job, and decided to take off. She said she always wanted to see Egypt and I said "me too" though I didn't know I had the desire until she mentioned it. Denise, sleeping in the bed across the way, said she'd come too.

My mother had a cow when I told her we were going to Egypt. She talked about an authoritarian government and lack of medical care. My mother wanted me to get away from Dale and, now that I am, she still wants to control what I do. If my child is not with me, I'm going to do what I want.

We flew Egypt Air because it was the cheapest. Everybody smoked on the flight and I'm going to smell like a cigarette for the next few weeks. Not a filtered American cigarette, but the sharp, bitter ones that they smoke here. Already I sound like a tourist, complaining about the locals and their habits. I will try to get over that and be more open to local customs.

Anyway, we are in Egypt. We landed at Cairo Airport which is crowded and dirty. Had to get our visas which meant standing in line forever. A bunch of Japanese tourists, about thirty of them, were in line in front of us. Each one paid for their visa with a credit card and each one took forever to process. In the middle of the processing, the one sole person giving out visas goes to get a cup of tea. Another person comes in but says she can't do the visas, it's not her job. So, we all mill around until the man in the gallabiyah comes back, takes a sip of tea, and starts talking to people again. Gallabiyah, that's the long, usually white garment that the men wear. At least in the airport. Saw less of them when we left the airport. Most Egyptians dress in western garb, though there are occasional gallabiyahs and abaya (the long garment worn by women, usually black) to let you know you're not in Kansas.

Lots of children running around the street and getting underfoot. Little boys run in the streets and little girls sit with their mothers and talk or draw. Makes me miss my child that I will not see grow up.

I don't know what I expected. Sand and pyramids and camels, maybe. Cairo is a city with cars—though tiny cars—and freeways and billboards. Didn't see any desert but did spot an occasional camel, walking alongside the freeway.

The hostel is right in the center of the city. Rooms are small but cleaner than I expected. Peta, Denise, and I will share a room to save expenses and because they didn't want to rent a room to a single woman. Seemed like a fight we weren't going to win. We asked about food and were told the hospice only served one meal a day, between 7 and 9 pm. It was now after 11, so we missed it. The helpful clerk said that we could go to the market across the way and pick up something to eat. His English was marginal so we asked him several times if the market would be open so late. He assured us it would.

We went to check. The market was open and doing a thriving business. We ran into another student from the hospice, Carl, and he told us many Cairo businesses closed during the heat of the day and stayed open late at night. Carl said the market also delivered. Come to the market, pick out what you want and when you want it, and the market will deliver items on your schedule. Tips the courier about one Egyptian pound, or twenty-five cents. No more, or they would expect it from everyone.

It sounded like a great system, but it took a while to execute. First, we had to pick out the food we wanted, and the clerk set it aside for us. Then we had to go to the cashier who added up the goods and made out a receipt for what was owed. Then to the money handler who took the money. The last stop was the delivery coordinator who made up the schedule of what we wanted and when it was to be delivered. The entire process took almost a half hour, after we had picked out the food. Carl, our guide to things local, explained that there was little technology and much unemployment in Egypt. Therefore, most any service was provided by multiple people who worked cheaply. Some of the people in the store were related to the owner, as he was obligated to provide for his family. Others just needed jobs and could be fired at the whim of the owner. Most people did not fire their employees; they just hired more people to take up the slack. Nothing moved quickly in Egypt.

This sounded racist. Characterizing an entire culture as slow. Carl argued that it was just different. Egyptian culture valued consensus. Everybody belonged to a family, or a group, or they were nothing. The last meal of the day was served at seven or later because the family would discuss at length what they wanted to eat and where they should buy it. Nobody wanted to cause discord.

Outside the market, we were met by young, really young, about eight or ten years old, children. There were about a half dozen of them. It was now after midnight and I asked Carl what they were all doing on the street. He said that these were the street children. Belonging to a family was the reason for Egyptian identity and these children didn't have a family.

"Can't they become part of another family?" I asked. "If family is so important."

Carl hemmed and hawed and said it's complicated. Adoption is illegal in Egypt so the children couldn't officially become part of another family. I asked, so all these children have dead parents.

"No," said Carl and looked uncomfortable again. Islam allows multiple wives and the children belong to the father. Sometimes the father's new wife doesn't want the children of the previous wife and they end up on the street. Some were born outside of marriage. It's not supposed to be this way. Men aren't supposed to have multiple wives unless they can support all of them and their children. But poor people say it's a class thing and want many wives. This is what happens.

I had spent the last two months in Europe. Other than the language thing and occasional weird foods, the daily life seemed familiar. Frustrating, sometimes, when I couldn't read the street signs or I ate octopus, but familiar. This was a different culture with different values. I'd complained about too much Catholicism in France and Italy, now I was faced with none at all. Guess I'm never satisfied.

We made it back to the hostel, made up the beds, and I fell into mine. Don't remember anything else until eight the next morning, when Peta woke me up. It is strange; in Europe, I didn't sleep most first nights in a new place. We were scheduled to take a 9:30 a.m. flight to Aswan and then on to Abu Simbel. Peta insisted we could not go to Egypt without going to Abu Simbel, the temple that had been taken apart when the Aswan Dam flooded the valley and was reassembled in the south of Egypt. The thought at the time was that it would bring tourism to southern Egypt. Now there was a civil war in Sudan, and nobody could go to the temple except by air or by heavily guarded caravan. We decided against the caravan when we were told that you couldn't leave the carriage.

Just before we left, the bell in my room rang. I pressed the buzzer to acknowledge that I was in and went to the end of the hallway to the phone booths. I called the reception desk and gave my room number, the only thing in English some receptionists could recite. When I was connected, my mother said, "Amythyst, is that you? I've been trying so hard to reach you."

I hung up on her and went to pack.

At the last minute, Carl decided he would come with us. He said there were always air tickets available at the last minute. He was right. We boarded another Egyptian Air flight, with everyone having their morning cigarette.

And made another discovery. The plane that we were on flew from Cairo to Abu Simbel, with a twenty-minute stop in Aswan. However, when we asked for tickets, we got on a flight from Cairo to Aswan, got off this plane, waited an hour, and then boarded another plane to Abu Simbel. When we asked, we were told that we could not remain on this plane to Abu Simbel, though the plane was not full. And we have no confirmed reservation back to the Aswan; that reservation would have to be made in the airport at Abu Simbel. Because we had checked out of the Cairo hostel and intended to stay in Aswan, we were dragging our luggage with us through the airports and, it looked like, through the ruins at Abu Simbel. I was cursing Peta, who made the reservations. She pointed out that she didn't know the procedure either and just followed the advice of the person at the Cairo hostel.

I closed the diary. Funny how it opened to my arrival in Egypt. I'd forgotten how angry I was with my mother and how naïve I was about my life. The toughest thing I had to do was get on a scheduled air flight. My emotions were more raw then, before they got rounded off in law school. Now, I thought before I spoke, most of the time, and my life was not so dramatic.

I liked my calmer, more predictable life, but enjoyed reading about the younger, more impulsive me.

I heard a mewing sound and some scratching. I opened the door to the basement and Bronte, my mother's cat, flew into the kitchen. She went to her bowl and howled. I filled her bowl and her water dish and she ate like she'd never seen food before. At least I could cross finding the cat off my to-do list.

SUNDAY

I DREAMED OF THE DESERT. MILES AND MILES OF SAND. HOT, and yellow, and much nearer the equator than New Hampshire. I knew I was dreaming but couldn't stop. Then I was awake.

And in my mother's house.

It was seven in the morning but I didn't feel rested. I got up, took a shower, and got dressed. Still only seven thirty. I decided to go downtown and sit in a coffee house and drink coffee. There had to be early risers in Keene; something had to be open. I gathered up my purse and my phone and my keys and opened the front door.

Dale was standing on the front porch, holding a cardboard tray with two coffees and a bakery bag. It appeared something was open.

"Carol always went out for breakfast so I thought you probably needed supplies." He held up the bakery bag. "I didn't get in until late and I know there's no food in the house."

I continued to stare at him for a few more moments. A halo of dark roast surrounded us. I held the door in what I hoped was a welcoming gesture. Couldn't remember the manners book covering how to address your old flame who was now your mother's caretaker.

Dale entered the house and walked into the kitchen. He got our coffee cups and plates, like he'd done it hundreds of times before. Maybe he had.

He poured the coffee from the paper cups into a ceramic mug. "Carol always hated to drink from paper cups. Just a habit now." He put one of the ceramic mugs in front of me. I thought of Chloe and how she had done the same thing.

"I remember," I said. "She wanted real cups and real plates and to sit at the table to consume them."

I sat down, looking out the east window. The same chair I sat in when we ate at the table. This wasn't our home when I was a child, but I still didn't sit at the head or the foot.

Dale sat across from me. "I knew you were coming, but it was still a shock to see you." He didn't look shocked. A smile played at the corner of his mouth. "But it's great seeing you again. And I want to learn all about you and what you've been doing over the last decade or two."

"I'm married," I said.

"I know. The wedding ring sort of gave it away." He picked up my left hand and looked at the ring. "Besides, your mother always talked about your kids. Ash is going to college and the twins, Phil and Pam, are the brightest high schoolers in the universe."

That was a surprise. I never thought of my mother bragging about her grandchildren. When I was a teenager, she told me to call her Carol, so that others wouldn't know that she had a daughter that old. Carol embracing grandparenting was something I needed to get used to.

"And you're a judge that helps children," he continued. "And your husband runs all of the manufacturing in Massachusetts and wants you to be successful."

I smiled. "I guess my mother has given you the complete rundown, at least as she sees it." I took my hand from his. "Tell me about you."

"I've been married twice, no kids. I'm not a great husband; both wives left me for somebody who is around more. Mentally and physically." He got up from the table, got the paper bag, and put some pastry on to a plate. Set the plate between us. "Maybe I was just trying to replace what I had lost."

"What you lost?" I reached for a bear claw and took a bite.

"You," he said. "And the baby."

We were not having this conversation. Twenty years ago, we had produced a baby that I gave up for adoption. I liked to think of the child growing up in a big, white house with piano lessons and ballet lessons and a dog. A girl I had never seen. That image of our daughter, happy and cared for, got me through the hard times. We were not discussing it now.

"Do you ever think about our child?" Dale asked. "What happened to her?"

"No." I pushed the bear claw away. I'd lost my appetite. Picked up the mug and took a sip, just to have something to do.

"You don't ever think about her?" Dale took my hand again, this time the one without the ring. "About where she is and what she's doing?"

"No." Only every day of my life.

"She's twenty-one now," he said, as if I didn't know. "Maybe in college. Studying what? English literature? Biochemical engineering?"

"I don't want to talk about this. Not now, when I need to concentrate on my mother."

Dale stood up, picked up his plate and coffee cup, took them to the sink, and rinsed them out. It took me years to get Magda to do that. Somebody had put some time into house training him.

He turned around, leaned back against the sink, and put his hands on the counter behind him. "Have you ever thought of looking for her?"

"Who?" I asked. As if I hadn't heard the last ten minutes of the conversation.

"Our daughter," he said. "She's an adult now and I'd like to know how she's doing."

"I think I prefer the fantasy that she's living a happy, productive life."

"But you've thought about it." His statement wasn't a question. "So have I. I want to know whether she's smart, or talented, or happy. Not to interfere with whatever life she's living, just to know."

"You're serious about this?" I moved away from him. "Why?"

"Your mother has been talking to me over the last year. She regrets that she never got to know her first granddaughter. She brags about the other children, but she regrets that she didn't know our child."

"Have you forgotten that it's my mother who split us up? Who pressured me into giving up the child? And who sent me half a world away to get away from you?"

"I think that she regrets that," he said. "And I know I regret it too." He moved to stand closer to me. "Do you ever think about me?"

"Think about you?"

"Yes. What would've happened if we didn't split up? Maybe we would be living in a house with a garden and taking our daughter to college. And watching our other children grow up." He took a strand of my hair and pushed it off my face. "Do you think about that?"

All I could think about was him. He still smelled like musk and ink. No more tobacco smell, he must have quit that habit. My mother said to give him another chance.

"I have other things to think about. Like the children I'm raising now."

"You only knew him a few months when you married him. You were on the rebound from me."

"I knew Magda eight months before I married him. Magda's a good man and it was long enough." It seemed important to me that I keep saying his name, that I keep the connection to him.

"And you never thought of me?"

I stepped away from Dale. "We are not having his discussion."

He took his car keys out of his pocket. "I'm here to take you to the grocery store, because I know there is no food in the house."

"I've got my car. I don't need a ride."

I picked up my keys and left the house. Dale followed me out.

I went to the small local grocery store down the street and got bread, milk, yogurt, peanut butter, bananas, and some vegetables that had seen better days. This would get me started. I would hit the bigger market or the farmer's market on Thursday, if I was here that long. I went home, dropped off the groceries, and made my way to the hospital.

I tried to figure out how I was going to do this. Keene and Meredith were only about an hour apart; some people did that commute every day. I liked living near where I worked, but I could do the commute for a few weeks until things were settled with my mother.

Of course, that meant dealing with Dale and his unrealistic

ideas. I'd only been a juvenile court judge for six months, but as a lawyer, I'd worked in the system for years. Everybody has an individual response to bringing up the past, especially if it involved family. Speaking of family, it wouldn't be pleasant dealing with Magda if I was spending more time with Dale.

I'm not obsessive, but I like to go over all the possible contingencies. The fact that most of the things I worried about never happened and the devastating things I saw in my life were surprises didn't deter me from going over all the possibilities. But I needed to get on with my life.

Not a parking space to be found in the hospital lot, though it was just after nine. I jammed my car between two SUVs and hurried in.

When I walked into my mother's room, she was in bed. A woman in a white coat stood at the end of the bed. They were having a serious discussion with a handsome young man, blond hair and blue eyes, who was holding my mother's hand. It took me a moment to realize the man was Dale. He looked so much younger with my mother and he hadn't told me he intended to visit her.

Nobody paid any attention to me. I politely cleared my throat. My mother would have been proud of me, had she not been so engrossed in Dale.

The woman in the white coat turned around to look at me. She was several inches shorter than me, with flawless coffee-colored skin and heavy eye makeup. If I had to guess, I would say she was the dominant personality in the room. Quite an accomplishment with my mother.

My mother raised her head. "Dear, this is Dr. Josefson, sent to bully me into taking my meds." She beamed up at the man at her side. "And you know Dale."

He tossed his head back as he turned to me and that gesture brought it all back. The way I once felt about him, our child, and all the things I'd tried not to think about that morning at breakfast. The visual processing thing again. I could deal with him as another person in my mother's life, but the head toss brought up emotions.

Nobody was looking at me. Nobody said anything. I stepped further into the room and shut the door. Dr. Josefson murmured something, grabbed the door handle, and left. It closed behind her with a soft swish.

"What is going on here?" My years of legal training and being on the bench kicked in. I managed to get out the sentence without shouting. "But what are you doing here, now, with my mother?"

"I came to visit," he said. "I guess I got used to seeing Carol every day."

Because I wasn't around to see her every day. Not that I hadn't offered to bring my mother to Massachusetts to live with us. She could have come. She was retired, technically, though she still had a tiny office at Keene State. And she said her friends were here. Including the man she told me not to marry, who was now here in her hospital room and holding her hand.

My phone played the first few notes of "Ode to Joy." One of my kids.

"Hey." Ash's standard greeting. "How's Gramma?"

I gave the phone to my mother and she said a few words to Ash and asked about school. Seemed disappointed that he wanted to work with computers, not be an English major. She handed the phone back to me.

"Thanks, Ma, I'm glad I got to talk to Gramma." I heard

footsteps in the background. "Dad wants to talk to you."

"Abbi." It was Magda. "When are you coming home?"

That was the question. I had set myself up to oversee the kids, my husband, the house, and my mother. Now my mother had decided to look elsewhere for guidance and picked another man I had to negotiate with. Magda was waiting for an answer. I stepped out of the room into the hallway.

"I'll leave early in the morning and go directly to the court-house," I said. "I'll talk to you tomorrow night about what happens next."

"You make everything complicated," he said. "Just come home. And bring your mother with you. We can take care of her here."

He meant I could take care of her and them in the same place. It did make some sense, but I didn't want to have this conversation now.

I took the coward's way out. "I'll call you later." I disconnected the call before he could reply.

I didn't want to go back into the room. The corridor I was standing in was painted industrial green, with occasional land-scapes in wood frames. I headed toward the waiting room across from the nurse's station. I just wanted to sit down in a place without anybody I was related to there to ask me questions or make demands.

The men who occupied the waiting room earlier had left, replaced by an older couple who looked like they had been awake all night. Someone had made more of an effort in decorating this room. All soothing grays and earth tones. Comfortable cushions on the chairs, some magazines, and a TV tuned to a talk show in the corner. I sank into one of the upholstered chairs.

An older man in a fluorescent yellow vest came into the room.

"Would you like some coffee or a muffin?"

It took a few seconds for me to realize that he was talking to me. "Coffee?" I asked.

"Yes, ma'am." The broad face broke into a smile. "I'm Ralph, the hospitality volunteer. Is there anything else you need? A muffin? For me to call somebody? We have social workers on staff and clergy on call."

Maybe I looked worse than I thought. "Coffee would be good, Ralph," I said. "Black."

Ralph went off to wherever the coffee lived. I listened to the talk show for a few minutes. Some politician had said something stupid; some election was taking place somewhere. Nothing new.

"Ah, there you are." I was expecting Ralph, but Dale spoke from the doorway. "I thought you might have left the hospital."

"No, just trying to gather my thoughts."

"About me?" Dale sat down beside me. "Or about your mother?"

"Both, I guess." I leaned back in the chair. It really was comfortable. "My mother seems to lean on you."

"I was available," said Dale. He must have realized how that sounded. "You have a family and obligations in Meredith. I'm in Keene and it made sense for me to move in with your mother. She's been editing my books and I do the cooking and cleaning. She has some students she's mentoring over once a week, so that's the only time I really need the house to look good. After six months, we've worked out a mutual existence."

"I do appreciate what you're doing," I said. "I read some of your books. I liked them."

"Please tell your friends and write a positive review." Dale looked at me. "I went to a conference where they told us to say that every time someone compliments your work. It's sort of a reflex now. But I'm doing okay, making some money. Not enough to live on my own, but the arrangement with your mother suits both of us."

I realized I never knew how they reconnected. "So, did my mother just call you up one day and ask you to come help her?"

"No." Dale shifted in his seat. "I belong to the local Citizen Advocacy group. Your mother came looking for someone to help her through the insurance paperwork, I was there, and we got to talking. I'd just started on my MFA and she offered me the room upstairs." He handed me a card, with his name, address, and phone number on it.

Citizen Advocacy. Until a few days ago, I didn't know there was such an organization. Now I had met two people claiming to be members.

"Citizen Advocacy. I've heard of that before."

"You have?" He sounded surprised. "It's international, but each group is very locally based. New England, Georgia, Nebraska, Australia, Canada."

"I met a member in Massachusetts."

Dale chuckled. "We don't have membership cards or dues. But we do have a Massachusetts chapter. Just local people trying to help. I'm helping out your mother."

"I thought my mother hated you."

The smile vanished from his face. "She doesn't hate me. She just didn't want me to marry you. Thought I wasn't good enough."

"But you're good enough for her?"

"She's known me almost thirty years. Read the stuff I've written. I had the skills and knowledge she needed. Maybe she remembered the good times and wanted to forget the rest."

"That's a lot to forget."

While I was talking, Ralph had come into the room and put the cup of coffee on the side table. It was in the smallest size possible and only three-quarters full. I took a sip. And it tasted like industrial coffee, thick and bitter. At least it was hot. I took a few more sips.

Dale and I walked back to my mother's room.

My mother picked at the sheet with the tips of her fingers. "Guess you want to talk," she said. "Dale hasn't taken your place."

"I don't think that's what she meant," said Dale.

"It may not be what she meant, but it was what she was thinking," said my mother. "I'm good at subtext."

That was my mother's standard English professor joke, but I didn't think it was very funny right now.

"You're still on all the bank accounts and Dale has promised not to make any decisions without talking to you. You are still my health care proxy and my power of attorney."

My mother cleared her throat and continued. "Those people who came to get me overreacted. There was no need to call you. It was a hit and run."

"The police came to talk to me," said Dale. "I told them I had no idea why you were out walking, alone, so early in the morning."

"They talked to me, too," said my mother. "I told them I went out to get Bronte."

"Bronte? The cat?" asked Dale. "She never goes outside. Wouldn't know what to do there."

"That's what I told the 'Mr. Johnson,' who called me. He insisted Bronte was at his house and he got my phone number from her collar. I'd figured she'd be frightened and he said he was just two houses away. I hope he's taking care of her. Or that guy in the maroon van didn't hit her."

"Bronte wasn't outside," I said, at the same time Dale asked, "What van?"

My mother looked from one of us to the other. She decided to answer Dale's question. "The maroon van that passed me. It was going like the hammers of hell." Leave it to my mother to get in a literary illusion when talking about a hit and run.

"Did you tell the police about the van?" asked Dale. "Is that what hit you?"

My mother shook her head. "I didn't remember the van until just now. It might've hit me. I don't remember. And Mr. Johnson said Bronte was outside."

"He wasn't," I said. "He was trapped in the basement. I let him up last night."

"Bronte was in the house?" asked my mother. "Then why did Mr. Johnson call me?"

"I'd like to know that too," I said. "What's his full name and where does he live?"

"I don't know him at all," my mother replied. "The houses are all set back, it's not like we can talk over the back fence. I'd never heard of him until he called. His phone number is probably still on my caller ID."

Dale went to the tiny hospital locker and brought out a plastic bag with my mother's name on it. I could see the phone through the clear plastic.

Dale pulled out the phone swiped across its face. "You should have a password on this." He pressed and swiped some more. "Here it is, only one call on Saturday morning. I'll write it down." He took one of the scratch pads and pens by my mother's bedside.

How my mother managed to accumulate a stack of paper and pens in a hospital bed was a mystery for another time.

Dale looked at me. "I think we need to report this to the police. Will you come with me?"

I nodded and picked up my purse.

"Not so fast," said my mother. "When am I going to get out of here?"

"Ma, it's not going to happen that quickly."

"Why not?" She didn't seem to grasp her situation.

"Because it's a weekend and the social services people aren't even in the hospital. I may need to make arrangements for orthopedic rehab or for someone to come in and it's likely you'll need in-home services. It may take a few days."

"I don't want to wait a few days. Dale, tell her I want to go home now. You can take care of me."

Dale picked up a jacket laying on the chair. "Carol, you broke some bones and you need to heal. I agree with Abbi, we need to talk to social services tomorrow." He started for the door. "Is there anything you need before Abbi and I go to the police? I'll be back later."

Dale and I went to the police station. We discussed just calling, but I wanted to talk to a police officer about what was going on. Though it was a Sunday, Officer Strom, in charge of the investigation, was in. He led us to a conference room with padded chairs and a coffee maker.

We all sat down.

"What can I do for you?" asked Officer Strom.

"When we spoke to my mother this morning, we learned some disturbing information." I then told him about my mother's phone call, and my discovery of the cat. Dale told him about the maroon van. Dale gave him the piece of paper with Mr. Johnson's phone number on it.

"It seems suspicious that someone would call, lie to my mother to get her out of the house, and then she is involved in a hit and run." Nothing like stating the obvious. "What have you learned about what happened?"

"We were suspicious before you arrived," said the officer. "Your mother lives on a dead-end road that ends about a quarter mile after her home. At the end of the road is a Veterans of Foreign Wars clubhouse."

I nodded. I knew this. Dale remained silent.

"VFW has had some break-ins, so they installed closed circuit monitoring. We got the videos, or the downloads, or whatever you get from CCTV."

"And what did you find?" This from Dale, who seemed anxious for the officer to get on with his story.

"Only three cars went to the end of the road that early on Saturday morning. One of them had stolen plates. Strange though, the van with stolen plates went down the road but the CCTV doesn't record it coming back up the road. We went down to the end of the street and didn't find the van, so our guess is that the VFW installed a cheap system that doesn't work all the time."

"And you suspect that car hit my mother?"

"We are exploring the possibility. And now we can trace this number and see who called your mother and knew her cat was missing."

"That confuses me." One of many things that confused me. "How did the person know the cat was missing?"

"Lucky guess." Strom shrugged his shoulders. "Or somebody was in your mother's house and locked the cat in the basement."

"I'm staying in the house now. Mr. Cassidy lives there. Is it safe?"

"I'm getting the locks changed and a security system set up," said Dale. "I'll offer extra if they'll do it on Sunday."

"I'd still be careful." Officer Strom looked from me to Dale and back. "What is your relationship anyway?"

"I'm Mrs. Donnelly's caretaker and live in the house. Mrs. Hartwell is her daughter, visiting from Massachusetts." Dale spoke clearly and formally, a rarity for him.

Officer Strom stood up. "Be careful and I'll let you know if we get any more information."

We left. My mother was sleeping when we got back to the hospital. I read a magazine from three months ago and Dale got on his phone and attempted to get a locksmith and a security specialist to the house on a Sunday. For time and a half, the locksmith agreed to change the locks today. Despite financial incentives, the security company would not be available until Tuesday.

Toward the end of the visit, an aide brought a piece of paper to us, saying that the facility was having a "planning meeting" for my mother on Tuesday morning.

"They've scheduled a planning meeting for my mother." I put the notice in my purse. "Tuesday at ten thirty. Maybe we'll get some answers on what happens next."

"I'll be there," said Dale. "I have a list of questions about Carol's care." He sat up straighter in his chair. "I've thought about inviting Richard Paoletti to the meeting."

A few minutes ago, I didn't even know there was going to be a meeting. "Why Richard?"

"I've been talking to him about your mother and her care."

I must have shown my displeasure because Dale put out his

hand, as if to calm me.

"It was a professional consult," he continued. "Richard, because of his disability, has more knowledge of health care in New England than most people I know. He went to Dartmouth, so he had to negotiate the New Hampshire health care system too. He knows about resources I never thought of."

Lack of knowledge about resources for my mother would slow down the system. And I was cynical enough to know that the choices offered would be influenced by insurance, ease of transfer, and payment options. Having a neutral person with another perspective wouldn't be a bad thing. "Will he do it?"

"Only one way to find out." Dale took out his phone, called Richard, and explained the situation. The rest of the conversation, on his part, was not informative.

Dale put his phone in his pocket. "He's available on Tuesday morning. He'll try to arrange transportation but, if need be, I can go pick him up and bring him to the medical center."

I'd never considered how Richard got around in the community or out of state. "He doesn't drive?"

"He's got hand controls on his van and he can drive himself around town. Longer trips tire him and his parents insist on a driver. They have one on call, who knows Richard and his needs."

Dale's phone pinged. "Richard's arranged a ride. He'll be here."

I pulled my car into the garage, clear of clutter. The locksmith van followed me into the driveway.

Dale showed the locksmith the front and back doors and stressed that he wanted deadbolts on both. Both doors were heavy and insulated, so we would hear if someone tried to enter the house. The locksmith also suggested a slide bar on the French door in the living room. He got right to work. Dale left to go upstairs to his office.

It felt strange being in a house with Dale, even if the locksmith was there also. I decided to read some more of my diary while I waited.

Tonight was gallabiyah night. After dinner, everyone gathered for a party wearing the long, cotton garments that were traditional Egyptian dress. For men anyway. The women wore gallabiyahs also; I guess playing with tradition is playing with tradition. But I'm busty and the gallabiyahs available in Egypt are smaller and do not have darts. So, all night, I'm pulling the top of the gallabiyah into place. Nothing showed, but every time brought attention to my breasts.

Someone noticed. Robert—not Bob—an Englishman, raised his eyebrows every time I made an adjustment.

Let me go back a minute. It had been a tough day. Got up at sunrise to go to yet another temple. This is the third day. Our guide, whose name I forget, says that the best time to visit temples is early in the morning, before the heat of the day. So, for the last three days, we have been up at sunrise to go on a land tour. Temples with sandstone, with crocodiles, with winged Isis. Not that I can always tell when sunrise is; we have a room on the waterline. These rooms are cheaper that the upper decks and we spend most of the time on the barge in the dining room or out on the deck anyway.

Back to the story, we got up at dawn, went to the temple, came back to the boat, and spent most of the day waiting to go through the locks. Ships and barges were lined up along the Nile and allowed through on some schedule known only to Allah. So, lots of time to sit on the deck and think. And have a few drinks.

The drinks did me in. I become sentimental and started thinking about Heather. That's what I decided to call my child. Heather. It gives images of blond hair and running across meadows. Besides, I couldn't keep calling her "the baby." Someday she will be six and go to school and then sixteen and go to prom and twenty-six and get married. And I won't see any of it. Because I wasn't strong enough to stand up to my mother and say that I wanted to keep my child. My child. Being raised by strangers. Just sent her out into the world and let her be raised by someone I don't even know.

So, by the time of the gallabiyah party I was in a fine mood; my eyes were red from crying, and I was exhausted. Peta talked me into going. Said it would make me feel better.

It didn't. And now I had Robert eyeing me every time I adjusted the damn costume.

Of course, he came over.

"Having problems with the gallabiyah?" he asked. His British accent made the question sound sexier than he meant it. At least, that's what I told myself.

"No problem," I said. I'd been lying to myself a lot lately.

He stepped closer. He smelled like cigarettes and whiskey.

He suggested we go out on the deck and I followed him out. It was better there. The sun had set and the Nile lay dark and quiet around us.

"What are you doing in Egypt?" he asked.

Not a very original pick-up line.

I told him I was on vacation, a break from college. No

mention of a child or a pushy mother. Or of Dale, who I was missing more than I wanted to admit.

Robert launched into a long, convoluted story about his important job and how he was lending his construction expertise in a place called Dubyae. Never heard of it.

"What are you building there?" I asked.

"Everything," he said. "They need roads and buildings and shopping malls."

I tried to imagine a place without shopping malls. Even Egypt had some of those. Robert explained that the ruler of Dubyae had found oil and they were building cities. Maybe I would put that on my list of places to go.

Robert stepped closer. Suggested that we go inside, as the breeze was picking up on the deck. It was breezy.

I followed him inside. He walked through the main hall, where gallabiyah clad people were playing some sort of trivia game. Kept walking to a cabin on the top deck.

"We can talk in here," said Robert. "It's quieter."

The room was twice the size of ours and had a great view. I knew the upper decks were not terribly expensive, just beyond our budget. There were twin beds in this room, too, though it looked like only Robert stayed here.

He pulled out a flask. Silver, with a thistle on it. I asked him if it was a family heirloom. He laughed and said his family built ships in Liverpool until the ship builders moved out. Poured us both a drink. It burned going down. Guess good whiskey didn't mean not burning. And Robert told me it was good whisky; better than was available on the ship.

We sat in chairs by the window and watched the Nile flow by. Had some more drinks. Kissed. Lay down on the bed.

I didn't object.

I hadn't had sex since Dale left, when I was pregnant. Over a year. I tried to pretend he was Dale. But Dale was younger and sweeter. I'd gone on birth control just after Heather was born, so even the danger of illicit sex was absent. I tried to remember Dale sneaking into my room, diving under the covers, and exploring each other. I miss Dale.

Robert wasn't Dale. We had sex. I didn't feel much. I made my excuses and left.

Maybe it was the sex, maybe it was the whiskey, but I slept soundly that night. When they came to get me for the temple tour the next morning, I waved them away and went back to sleep. Didn't appear on deck until lunch.

We have assigned seats at all meals. Guess the staff wants to keep track of us at least twice a day for lunch and dinner. I sat at my assigned table, with Peta and Denise and Carl. Played with my food.

"So, you came in late last night," said Peta.

"Yup."

"And you left with that dish, Robert."

"Yup."

Peta put down her fork. "I want details," she said.

I told her she wasn't going to get them and got up to leave. Ran smack into Robert.

"I've been looking for you," he said.

We decided to walk on the deck. It was sweltering. Now I see why we do tours in the early morning.

"I don't want to stay out here long," I said. "I've got things to do."

"Like pack," Robert said.

"We don't get to Luxor until tomorrow. And then I just transfer from the boat to an inn. Twenty minutes, tops. I don't have much stuff." I realized I was rambling and shut up.

"Or you could pack your things and come with me to Dubai."

I'd looked it up this morning and finally found it and the correct spelling—it's Dubai, not Dubyae. I was thinking about my new-learned geography and didn't realize for a minute what he was saying.

"Come with you?" I asked.

"Sure," he said. "It'll be great. You can come live with me in Dubai, we'll get something called a provisional marriage license and set up housekeeping."

I was so stunned I didn't say anything.

He went on to say how he was ready for a new phase in his life. We had an instant connection. The sex was great. Why not try out marriage?

I didn't feel an instant connection. And I barely remember the sex. Was he talking about last night? How much did I have to drink?

I walked by him into the dining hall, strong-armed Peta into walking with me, and went back to our room and shut the door against Robert and his plans.

"All finished." My reading was interrupted by the locksmith.

I closed the diary. "Let me go check with Dale, make sure there isn't anything else he wants you to do."

Dale agreed that we'd done what we could for the night. The security people would be here Tuesday.

"Let's walk down to the end of the road," I said. "Get some

fresh air."

"The air is no less fresh in the house, and it's getting dark." Dale pulled on his jacket. "But let's walk and talk."

I got to the end of the driveway and turned toward the dead end of the street. I wanted to check out something. Dale followed me.

We walked in silence for a few minutes. It was quiet out here, even the traffic sounds were muffled.

Dale kicked a stone to the side of the road. "So, have you thought any more about what I said this morning?"

I kept walking.

"I think we should try to find our daughter. She's out there and she's a part of us. I think we should make contact and see what she says."

My mind drifted to my conversation with Niagara. She so wanted to connect with her brother and it felt like he wanted the same. What if Heather was out there looking for me?

"I don't know." That's all I said.

Dale took hold of my arms and turned me to face him. "Sometimes you've got to face your fears. See what happens. Open up your horizons."

"But I have a good life." It seems I was destined to repeat conversations with the important men in my life. "I have a husband and children and a job I'm good at."

"You could have another child in your life. One that may be looking for you." Dale took a half-step closer to me, so there was no air between us.

"Or I could disrupt everything I've worked for. What if Heather has a great life and doesn't want to see us? What if she's needy and clingy?"

"What if, what if. What if she's a great addition to your life, your kids love her, and you're not taking the chance and seeing her?"

I stepped away from Dale and walked further down the road. Dale hurried to catch up with me. "Will you think about it?"

I nodded, and kept walking.

"We were good together, you and I," said Dale.

I stopped walking. "That was a long time ago."

"Not that long for me." Dale kissed me.

The kiss reminded me of hope and connections and the power of taking chances. Things I had set aside years ago. He deepened the kiss and I let him. I wanted to be reminded of a time when all things seemed possible, when I trusted everyone and believed that I would be successful and taken care of, no matter what I did.

I backed away from Dale. And kept walking down the road. I didn't intend to share any of my thoughts with him. We passed the VFW and came to the turn-around at the end of the road. The woods came almost up to the road and two blue dumpsters filled the grassy space to the right. A huge pile of brush was stacked next to the dumpsters. I went over to the brush.

"What are you looking for?" asked Dale.

"Why is this pile of brush here? If they were going to throw it away, why not put it in the dumpster?"

"Dumpsters are expensive. Maybe someone is coming to get the wood. To burn in their stove, or something."

That made sense, but the placing and stacking of the wood seemed strange. "There used to be a logging road here, right where the brush pile is." I walked around the pile. "You can see it here, and something heavy has driven over it recently. There's ruts in the mud." During mud season in New England, the ruts ran deep.

I walked along the side of the road, trying to save my shoes from the mud. If I'd known I intended to walk in the woods, I'd have worn my rubber boots. Dale followed me, but didn't seem very enthusiastic.

"Where are you going?" he asked. "It's getting darker."

"Just want to see what's down here," I said. "It's strange that they'd pile brush in front of a road that's been used recently."

About two hundred yards into the woods, the logging road took a sharp left turn. I stood at the corner and there it was. A maroon van, without plates, covered with brush and mud.

Dale came up behind me. "How did you know it was here?"

"I didn't." I suspected, but I didn't know. "But the police said the van didn't return down the road and it had to go somewhere. I didn't want to tell them about the road until I was sure." I walked up to the van.

"Don't touch it," said Dale. "It's evidence."

I shot him my best "I'm a judge, you idiot" look. It didn't even register with him.

"I'm just looking in the window." No need to tell him my thoughts. I don't know much about vans, but even I could tell this model was at least fifteen or twenty years old. It was battered and the inside was spartan. The seats had been patched with duct tape and the floor was metal. A cup holder was attached to the side of the seat; it contained some coins and what looked like horse chestnuts. Horse chestnuts produced nuts in the fall, not the spring, and only a few trees still survived in the town. Don't remember where I'd read that, but I did recognize the nuts. Nothing else on the seat, or the floor, or the dashboard.

"I guess we'll have to call the police again," said Dale.

Within twenty minutes, the area of the turn-around held two police cars and a tow truck. Everyone was waiting around while pictures were taken and the area searched before the van could be towed. Officer Strom, politely but firmly, escorted us back to my mother's house and told us he would contact us later.

Dale and I went back to the house. I wait very quietly and spent most of the time pacing the floor. After an hour and a half, the tow truck came by the house with the van on it. I grabbed the flashlight and headed for the door.

"Where are you going?" Dale didn't get up from the couch where he was calmly watching television.

"I'm going to see what's happening. They just took the van away."

"It's dark out."

"That's why I've got a flashlight." I waved it at him and went out the door.

It was very dark on this side street with no streetlights. It got lighter as I approached the VFW; the outside lights were on and the parking lot was illuminated. A single patrol car blocked the entrance.

A young woman in a uniform got out of the car as I approached. "Can I help you, miss?"

"I'm the person who found the van. I thought somebody was coming to talk to me."

"Don't know anything about that." The officer stepped in front of me. "The search has been suspended for the night. They'll be back in the morning. I'm sure they'll contact you."

Looks like I wasn't going to get any more information tonight.

MONDAY

I WOKE EARLY ON MONDAY MORNING AND GOT OUT OF the house without waking Dale. I didn't want to discuss the scene last night, or our daughter, or my mother, or any of the other unpleasant things I was now associating with him.

I drove directly from my mother's house to the courthouse. As usual, Cally met me in the judge's lobby to give me a rundown of the day.

"Almost back to normal," he said. "Though, of course, without Jenna."

"Back to normal?" I echoed.

"Police are gone, crime scene tape is gone. We all miss her."

"I saw Chloe this weekend. A celebration of her life is scheduled for Wednesday night at the Academy of Music."

"I'll put up some flyers and send around an email." Cally looked down at my desk.

"Speaking of email, I have a posting for social media. I'll send it to you and you can get it to everyone in the courthouse." I was hopeless at social media and Cally had to approve all general postings, anyway.

"Good, that's good. I've got today's list. You're the motion judge again. And you need to finish the hearing that was interrupted by Jenna's death."

"Yes, Attorney Paoletti's last hearing. And the sixth time for motions this month. Not that I'm counting." I took the list from him and flipped the pages. "I guess it makes sense. I've missed several sessions this week."

"We all know you were close to Jenna and you're trying to help Chloe. I predict you have a few more days of leeway before somebody starts complaining. And everything's in place for Paoletti's going away party."

I sat down in the chair. "That's true. People try to be compassionate, but lawyers want hearings to go forward as scheduled."

Cally tapped my to-do list, in the center of my desk. "How do you know Dennis Raymond?"

"Dennis Raymond?" I looked down at the list. "Call Dennis Raymond" was on the top of the list; that meant it was the oldest item, not the most important. It took me a few moments to remember why I wanted information on him. He was the person Jenna called just before her death. "He's a real person? What do you know about him?"

"Yeah, he's real enough," said Cally. "Works for Ascend, the battered women's shelter. Also helped a couple of important witnesses disappear."

"Disappear?"

Cally stepped away from my desk. "That's the rumor. He helps battered women escape their batterers, but he also has connections to witness protection. Don't know about the truth of that. How do you know him?"

"He came up in connection with Jenna's death."

Cally looked surprised. Or worried. Or something.

"Unusual that I would have a piece of information you missed,"

I said. "Don't worry, the police know about it. I just want to talk to him." I picked up the phone on my desk. "Just give me a few minutes and we'll start the session."

I called Ascend and was connected to Dennis Raymond's voicemail. I left a message that it was about Jenna Jay.

I flew through the motion session. That left the hearing that had been interrupted by Jenna's death. It was Attorney Paoletti's last case before me. A sad thing, because he was a staunch advocate and a good attorney. A good thing, because he was going on to practice in the more lucrative area of personal injury law. And, as he no longer appeared before me, he could represent Ash in the upcoming hearing.

This morning, when I entered the courtroom, the children's mother was sitting at the counsel table with Attorney Paoletti. She had on a dark pantsuit and her hair had been cut and styled. If she hadn't been sitting with her attorney, I wouldn't have recognized that she was the same woman from last week. Didn't matter. No way was I sending the baby, with fractured ribs, home to a situation where she admitted she and her boyfriend were the only caretakers of the child.

The hearing was over by two, which was great timing, because we had planned a going away party for Attorney Paoletti.

Cally and Robert, the temporary clerk, had decorated the conference room. Jenna bought the decorations before her death; I remembered seeing them in her office. Silver balloons and a sign saying, "We'll miss you." Cally had picked up the cake Jenna ordered and a VISA gift card. Paoletti acted surprised, though it was hard to be secretive in the courthouse.

"Thank you so much for getting this together for me." Paoletti raised his glass. "Though it's too bad we can't have alcohol in the courthouse. I'm going on to fame and fortune and a better life and I think we need spirits to celebrate the occasion."

"That would be appropriate," I said. "But having alcohol in the courthouse can get us all fired."

"Too bad." Paoletti looked around the room. "Though I know some people in this room have a bottle in their desks." His gaze stopped at Bert Rodgers, the older court officer. "For medicinal purposes."

Bert looked away from Paoletti and went over to the food table, studying its contents.

"Let's just all have a good time," Cally said. "Enjoy the food and the punch."

"Com…comradery is very important," said Paoletti. "Now I'm concentrating on personal injury, I'm relying on all of you to send me referrals from the courthouse."

"That would be a violation of courthouse rules." This from Bert Rodgers, still standing at the food table.

"And we wouldn't want to do that." Paoletti took a sip of his drink and spilled some of it on the front of his shirt.

I wondered if he'd started drinking before the party, though I hadn't noticed any problems while we were finishing the hearing.

"Red punch on your shirt doesn't look good on a high-earning attorney," said Bert Rodgers.

"Are you saying I'm not a good lawyer?" Paoletti put down his glass and went to stand in front of Rodgers.

What was wrong with these two? It seemed they took pleasure in goading each other.

"I didn't say that," said Rodgers. "But some people do."

"Who said that? Tell me." Paoletti took a step closer to Rodgers.

Cally stepped between them. "Calm down, both of you. This

is a party and we're supposed to be having a good time."

"Rodgers never liked me. He's always telling people I don't know what I'm doing." Paoletti was getting red in the face and his voice was getting louder.

Cally put a hand on Paoletti's arm. "Calm down and enjoy your party."

Paoletti shook him off and turned to face Cally. "What the hell do you think you're doing? Touching me? That's assault."

Cally loomed over both Paoletti and Rodgers, exuding calm and reason.

Paoletti picked up his glass. "You're right, I need to enjoy my party."

We all had more punch and cake. Someone persuaded Gerard to "say a few words."

"I don't know whether I can say a few words," said Gerard. "I'm a lawyer. But I will miss all of you and the juvenile court." He took a sip of his punch. "But I'll be making more money, and having more fun, doing personal injury work. People actually appreciate when you get them money for their injuries."

"And you don't have to spend all your time in court." This from an attorney in the back of the room.

"I'll still do some trial work," Gerard continued. "After all, you can't get decent settlements if the insurance companies think you never try anything. And I mean to get decent settlements."

The head of the bar association was giving Gerard his VISA card when my phone rang.

Dale said that my mother wanted to talk to me.

"About what? Getting out of the hospital?" I didn't relish driving to Keene for a repeat of that conversation.

"I don't know," said Dale. "She won't talk to me; says she

needs to say something to you. In person."

A quick phone call to Magda, to confirm that he was home and the grounded children were accounted for. Even Phillip chose to remain close to home. I told him I would call him when I got to Keene.

Carol was in bed when I got to the room, though it was only five. She probably had never been in bed so early in her life.

"Hi, Carol, how are you doing?" I went over and gave her a peck on the forehead. We are not a family for physical signs of affection, but it seemed right. She looked so frail and old in the hospital bed.

Her white hair had not been combed and was standing up in wisps above her forehead. The head of the bed had been raised, but she listed to the left and did not look comfortable. I adjusted her pillows and sat her upright.

"Thank you, dear," she said. "Are you here to take my temperature?"

"No, Ma, I'm your daughter Abbi."

"Abbi?" She looked around the room. "My daughter is Amythyst Basil. Isn't that a lovely name?"

"Yes, it is a lovely name." I brought a chair near her bed and sat down. "But I'm a judge now and I go by A.B. or Abbi."

"Oh. Abbi. Oh, yes, you're the mother of Ashroff, Pam, and Phillip. How foolish of me." She stared out the window.

"Has Dale been in to see you today?"

"Yes, Dale, he's a wonderful young man. I'm so lucky that he is around."

"But I'm here now. And I'll take care of you."

"I know you will." She patted my hand. "You're a good girl."

"I try to do what's best." I looked out the window also, trying to see what held my mother's attention. Might as well ask her the questions now. "Ma, why is Dale living with you and taking care of you?"

She turned to look at me. "Because he was here. And I trust him."

"But why Dale? You tried to keep us apart. And the baby."

"The baby. That was a mistake." Carol turned to stare out of the window again. "When am I going home? I don't like it here. They don't know my routine and they stop me from getting out of bed."

"Ma, you were out walking and got injured. You said you wanted to talk to me tonight. What did you want to say?"

"Is that why my leg hurts?" She pushed the covers aside and looked down at her leg. A row of metal staples was lined up down the side. Two of them looked red and swollen and her right leg, the injured one, was noticeably larger than the left.

"Yes, I remember now,'" Carol said. "When are they going to take the staples out?"

"Your leg needs to heal some more. That's why you're in the hospital."

My mother smiled. "Hello, Dale."

I turned to see him in the doorway. And tried not to resent that he got a more enthusiastic greeting than I did.

"I come bearing gifts." Dale held up a paper bag, similar to the one he brought to the house. No coffee though.

I was not disappointed. Yes, I was. I could use some decent coffee right now.

Dale put the bag on her rolling table. "I got the eclairs you like from the Second Street Bakery."

"Yes, the one on Fifth Street." My mother's eyes sparkled at the old joke. The bakery had changed locations several years ago, but retained the same name.

"How are you doing?" Dale asked my mother.

She launched into a story about the follies of physical therapy and a Russian nurse who thought Carol was her long-lost grandmother. Dale got much more information about her day and her experiences than she gave to me.

"Ma, when was the last time that someone checked on you?" I asked.

"Why, you're checking," she said. "Do you want to take my temperature?"

"No, I'm not your nurse, I'm your daughter, Abbi."

"My daughter's name is Amythyst. Isn't that pretty? Amythyst Basil."

"Yes, it's a pretty name," I agreed. What choice did I have? "And I am your daughter."

"It was nice of you to come visit me, dear. Could you fluff up my pillows?"

I adjusted the pillows, once again propping her upright. My mother smiled at me.

Further conversation was interrupted by the clang out in the hallway. An aide ran the medication cart into the wall.

"What's that noise?" my mother asked. "Did that clumsy intern, Sally, drop something?"

Sally had been an intern back when she was teaching full time, over fifteen years ago.

The aide stopped the unwieldy cart outside the door, and took out a paper cup with some pills in it. She put it on my mother's bedside table.

"I've got to go the bathroom." My mother addressed the remark to the aide.

"Abbi and I will go down to the cafeteria for a few minutes." Dale took my arm and we started for the door. "She looks like she could use some coffee. Do you want some, Carol?"

"I don't know what I want. I'm just so tired." Carol stared out the window again.

I looked at my mother. She looked gray and about to nod off at any minute.

"Okay, let's go get coffee," I agreed. "Maybe we can get some fruit or something for her to eat later."

The cafeteria was stainless steel and fluorescent lighting. Though it was after the dinner hour, several groups of hospital employees were eating or having discussions over the remains of their food. A sign on the wall said the special was roast beef. Dale ordered coffee for both of us. I grabbed an orange from the fruit bowl for my mother. The bananas were brown and the apples suspiciously shiny.

When we sat down, I realized I was exhausted and hungry. I ate the orange without tasting it. The coffee was thick and dark and quite good for cafeteria food.

"Are you not talking to me?" asked Dale.

"No, I'm just hungry and tired. Carrying on a conversation at the same time seems like too much effort."

"So I'll talk. Your mother seems confused, and I'm still not sure how much care she'll need when she's released. Do you want me to stay in the house and care for her? Or do you want to take her to Massachusetts to be nearer to you?"

I took a pad of paper and a pen out of my purse. After all that happened, I was still my mother's daughter. "Let's make a list of questions for tomorrow. We can discuss options after we get the answers."

"Still keeping lists, Abbi?" Dale put his hand over mine, a reminder that he knew me well. Or, at least, knew the me of twenty years ago.

"The list." I wasn't going to discuss my habits, good or bad. "We'll need to know her diagnosis, her prognosis, and what options we have for her care."

"And we need to know what will happen if we do nothing."

"Do nothing?" That option hadn't even occurred to me.

"Yes." Dale smiled. "I teach decision making to my students. Many of them want to change the world, and take on myriad projects at the same time. I help them set priorities. The first question is, what happens if you do nothing? If that's acceptable, stop there."

My world of case lists and to-do lists and schedules didn't often have room for doing nothing as an acceptable alternative. Maybe I still have some things to learn from Dale. I added "do nothing" to the list of questions.

"I'm going to call Richard tonight," said Dale. "I'll ask him if he has any other things he's found out about her insurance or if there's anything else we need to know. Especially about transferring your mother from New Hampshire to Massachusetts, if that's our decision."

He stood up, picked up the remains of the meal from the table, and swaggered over to the busing station.

What if my mother can't go home? Not that I hadn't thought about it, but my mother had always been so self-reliant. I didn't look forward to that conversation with Magda. Bringing my mother to Massachusetts would mean I could oversee her care.

And it would change our relationship. Damn, I'm tired.

Dale came back to the table. "There's an atrium, with plants and a walking trail." He motioned toward the door. "Want to join me? It might do us both good."

"Is this another attempt to get me alone to talk about things I don't want to talk about?"

"Don't be so suspicious, Abbi."

I cringed at his familiarity and his damn smooth manner.

"I was just suggesting a pleasant walk before we have to go back and deal with the hospital again."

I stood up. "You're right, I would like to take a walk before we go back." I followed him out the door.

The atrium was pleasant, if obviously not natural. A smooth walkway meandered through artificial rocks and well-groomed greenery. Careful care was taken not to have uneven trails, or soil and mud on the walk. The illusion of the natural world without its messy parts.

Dale kept his word and we walked without talking. An older couple made frequent stops on the path but, other than the two of them, we were alone.

Dale's phone seemed extremely loud when it rang. The classic ring was that of a landline, forty or fifty years ago. The older couple frowned, as if in disapproval.

Dale glanced at his phone, then at me. "Excuse me." He stepped off the walkway path and into a grotto with a bench.

I continued to stroll the path, assuming he would catch up to me after the call. The atrium seemed to reflect the tastes of several different gardeners. The grotto where Dale stood contained a water fountain and a wooden bench. Other side paths were strung with tiny white lights and plastic statues that looked like stone to the casual passerby. There was definitely a concerted effort to look natural and not planned.

I heard my phone. Magda, no doubt with some other problem for me to solve. I thought of ignoring his call, but he would just call back later. I answered.

"How's it going?" He started in without even saying hello.

"I'm at the hospital now," I said. "They're still monitoring my mother and doing tests. Not much to tell."

"When are you coming home?"

It always come down to that question. I gave my standard answer. "I don't know."

"Why do you have to stick around the hospital? She's doing better."

"How do you know that?"

"I called the hospital, asked how she was. Said I was her daughter's husband. They told me she was resting comfortably and that you were in with her."

I didn't know whether to be comforted to think that he called about my mother or to be freaked out that he was checking on me. Stick to the facts.

"She's still my mother," I said. "And Dale keeps me informed."

"Yeah, Dale, of the twice weekly calls. I'm not sure I like the idea of you spending time with him."

"He's an old friend of the family. My mother has known him for years."

"Maybe you should stay, just to make sure he does right by your mother. But we all miss you."

"I miss you too." I realized it was true.

"Well, I'm calling you with some good news." Magda hesitated.

Why did he hesitate to deliver good news? Only one way to

find out. "What news?" I asked.

"I spoke to Attorney Paoletti about Ashroff. Seems we drew a judge who's big on family preservation. Ash may get off with pretrial probation, some classes, and then a dismissal. If the DA doesn't dismiss the charges outright."

"That is good news. So, will this show up on his record?"

"We need to talk about that. Paoletti says we can get the record sealed, but that may cause more problems than it solves."

"He's right," I replied. "Sometimes it's better just to let the dismissal stand. If an employer sees a sealed record, they could imagine a much worse situation that it actually was. Happens all the time in juvenile court."

"We can talk about that when you get home. Thought I'd let you know things are looking good, though."

"Thanks. I've got to go, get back to my mother."

"Love you." Magda was gone.

I stared at the soothing waterfall. I needed some good news in my life.

I heard hurried footsteps behind me and turned. Dale was running on the path; the older couple turned and frowned at him. When he got to me, he stopped and took a few deep breaths.

"This isn't a jogging path." Okay, a sick attempt at humor, but I was trying.

"Abbi." He didn't even grin, just took another deep breath. "It's about your mother."

"What about my mother?"

"There's a problem. They want us in the room. Now."

He turned and walked away for a few steps. "Are you coming with me? It's important."

I stood frozen on the path. Horrible images flashed through

my head. "How do you know it's important? What did they tell you?"

He came back to me, linked my arm with his, and started walking, pulling me along with him. "Let's go to her room," he said.

I followed him with weighted feet, my dread growing with each step. Not about anything specific, just a gray, lingering dread.

When we reached my mother's room, the curtains were drawn around her bed. A few bits of material littered the floor. The heart monitor was beeping steadily, a good sign. I pushed aside the curtain.

A nurse stood at the head of my mother's bed. A single nurse. If this was important, where were the other people who should be taking care of her? The nurse stepped back and I saw my mother. Or I saw the person on the bed who was supposed to be my mother.

She was gray. Gray hair, gray skin, and that gray lingering dread. I walked up to the bed and touched her. Her skin was warm.

"Your mother had a stroke," the nurse said. "She's been stabilized, but we need to get her to the critical care unit."

A stroke? My mother had a stroke? But she had been eating and talking to Dale and me less than an hour ago.

I sunk down in the chair next to the bed. I felt the wetness on my face, though I didn't remember starting to cry. Everything was the same. The white sheets, the smell of human bodies and cleaning products, the trees in bloom outside the window. But everything was different.

"Will she be okay?" I asked.

"We can't tell right away," said the nurse. "She's stable, but we don't know how the stroke has affected her functioning. We're going to run some more tests, get her to the critical care unit, and assess what to do next. It's unlikely we'll have any further information until the morning."

The nurse adjusted some plastic tubing and smoothed out the sheet. "Do you want me to notify anyone else?"

I had no idea how to answer that question.

"I've already done it." Dale joined us. "She's here now, just behind you."

Entering the room was a woman, not much taller that my five foot six, with a flowing purple dress and gray-streaked hair. She clutched a Bible and carried a huge floral handbag.

Dale made the introductions. Her name was Eudora Johansson-Flora and she was a minister at the local Methodist church. I never thought my mother went in much for organized religion. Maybe this woman was Dale's minister.

She took both my hands. "You must be Carol's daughter," she said. "She talks about you all the time. Let's go sit down."

She led me back to the seat in the corner and the three of us sat down. The nurse left.

"Do you want to talk about your mother or would you prefer to just sit here for a while?" The minister arranged the purple drapes of her dress.

What was I supposed to call her? What was supposed to happen next? I had no experience with medical emergencies. In the courtroom, they were abstract decisions to be made on strangers. Now I was in charge and I had no idea what to do.

"Call me Dora." Dora patted my hand.

That took care of what to call her. Just left were questions about what to do.

"Dora, I don't know what to do or what is expected of me. This is all strange to me." I started crying again halfway through the statement. Thankfully, Dora and Dale just sat back and let me cry. I didn't want anyone touching me or comforting me at the moment.

I stared at my mother. She was gray. The gray hair, gray skin, gray lips. Even the sheets seemed to have a gray sheen on them. This wasn't my mother, who was always talking and coming up with new ideas. What the hell was I doing sitting here anyway? There must be something I should be doing.

"I think your mother was greatly comforted by our church family over these last few years." Dora reached out to touch me, then withdrew her hands. I must have been giving off "don't do it" vibes.

"I wasn't aware that my mother was attending church regularly," I said. Not that I cared, but talking beat crying.

"Oh, yes, she is on the mission committee. She and the older ladies of the church knit hats and scarves for less fortunate children in the community."

I couldn't picture my mother attending church, doing missions, or knitting. The doubt must have showed on my face, because Dora plucked her phone out of her floral bag.

"I have pictures of your mother with the children," she said. "Carol does so love the little ones." She fiddled with the phone, turned it sideways, and showed me several pictures. Pictures of the woman I remembered, not the gray one on the bed beside us. She was with other white-haired ladies holding babies. All the babies had multi-colored caps and blankets.

I didn't know what to say, so I kept quiet. My mother, who couldn't wait for me to grow up so that she could talk to me and convince me she was right in all things. The woman who stayed in a hotel when she came to Massachusetts because my children "were so disruptive." It was only after all the children were teen-agers that she agreed to stay at the house, though her room was on the third floor and the children were on the second.

"Doesn't she look happy?" asked Dora.

I agreed, because it seemed important to her that I think so.

"I think I'm going home now." I stood up.

Dora and Dale stood also.

"Don't you want to spend more time with your mother?" asked Dora.

"Are you going to Massachusetts or will you stay at your mother's home?" asked Dale.

I decided to answer both questions in one sentence. "The nurse said they won't have any further information on my mother tonight. So, I'll stay at her house and come back in the morning to see what needs to be done."

"I'll go notify the nurse." Dale left, leaving me alone with Dora.

"We all grieve in our own way," said Dora. "You do what feels right. Do you want me to come back to the house with you?"

I thought of the house, with all my mother's things in it, and started crying. Dora came up to me and hugged me. My tears splattered on her purple dress. I wasn't sure that's what I wanted, but it didn't feel bad. She stepped back and offered me a tissue.

I blew my nose. Loudly. Dora didn't seem to mind. Probably saw a lot of this.

"I need to think about things," I said. "And I need to call my husband. Please excuse me."

I left without any more conversations with Dora or Dale.

My mother's house was unnaturally quiet. Or maybe it was me, knowing she would probably be changed by the stroke. Her clothes were still stacked on the dryer, her dishes were drying in the rack.

I had put off calling Magda long enough. The phone was picked up on the first ring.

"Abbi, how are you doing?" Magda was out of breath, as if he had run to the phone.

"Not well." I started sobbing and had to stop to blow my nose.

"What's going on? How can I help?"

"You can't help," I said. "My mother had a stroke this afternoon."

"A stroke? I thought she was getting better and you were making arrangements to come home."

I started sobbing again.

"I'm sorry, that came out wrong. What can I do for you?" he said. "Do you have someone with you? What is the prognosis for your mother?"

"My mother is still unconscious. They won't know anything until she wakes up." I realized I was rushing my words and took a deep breath. "I don't think you can do anything. They'll have more information in the morning, so I'm going to stay until then."

"Why don't you call one of your mother's friends? You shouldn't be alone."

"Dale is on his way home. He stopped to talk to the nurse, but he'll be here soon."

"Dale. I'm not sure that Dale is the person you should have with you." Magda was silent for several seconds. "Do you want me to come to Keene?"

"Magda, don't try to fix this. You stay there and take care of the kids. I'll let you know what happens next."

Silence for thirty seconds. A long time in a phone call. Then he said, "I'm sorry. Let's start over. Do we need to make arrangements for her to come live with us? Or near us?"

"We may need to have that conversation, but let's see what the doctor says tomorrow. Right now, I just want to go to sleep."

"Don't worry about me and the kids, I'll take care of that." I could depend on him in an emergency. "I'll make arrangements here. You take care of the arrangements there." I heard him say something but couldn't make out the words.

"What did you say?" I asked.

"Pam's here. Wants to know what's going on. Telling the kids is on me. You take care of yourself. Love you." And he was gone.

When my dad died, Carol and I drank wine and ate cheese and crackers. Carol said it was a fitting tribute. I was only fourteen years old. But it wasn't even my first drink, but the first time I drank half a bottle. Carol thought it was her duty to introduce me to alcohol, to "take away the mystique of the forbidden."

I walked through the house in a dream-like state. Found Carr crackers and Boursin cheese, just like when my dad died. In the back of the pantry, I found a bottle of raspberry merlot from a local winery. I poured myself a drink in the largest glass I could find.

My diary still lay on the nightstand. I decided to read about other times. Why not, wine, cheese, and musty memories. Good for the soul.

Back in Cairo and the youth hostel. Peta is still complaining about the cost of the flight to Abu Simbel and how little time we got to spend there. I pointed out that we had a lovely sail on the Nile and we got to explore the Old Cataract Hotel where Agatha Christie wrote Death of the Nile. She complains about how reckless we were to give our bags to an unknown guide, though we did get them back.

In Cairo, we spend lots of time walking the streets and just looking at the daily life in the city. Went to the National Museum in Tahrir Square. To get to the museum, we had to cross five lines of traffic in a three-lane roadway. With an occasional donkey cart or camel thrown in. Another cultural experience.

Even for poor almost college students, transportation and sightseeing in Cairo was inexpensive. We decided to go to the Giza pyramids and ride the camels, to see the Sphinx, and to just wander the streets. As our discussion about what to do took up most of the day, we got a late start. I wanted to put together a schedule for our stay, but nobody was cooperating.

At last, we made a decision to go to the Cairo Tower. The Cairo Tower is in the heart of the city and allows a view of the Nile, the city, and its surroundings. We had looked into the price of getting a driver and a car for the entire day, but, as it was already late afternoon, we took a cab. Riding in a cab in Cairo is scary. The main thoroughfare had three marked lanes but the Egyptians and the tourists manage to get five lanes out of the situation. The cabs are tiny and do not look well maintained. These tin cans are on the road with diplomatic vehicles, trucks with undermined cargo, and an occasional donkey cart or camel. I usually just shut my eyes until we get wherever we are going.

The front of the Cairo Tower has some greenery and a few benches. We walked past and bought our tickets to the top floor. The top of the tower consists of a restaurant and a viewing deck. Peta was right. You could see all of Cairo from the top. Cairo the modern city, radiating out from the tower, and Old Cairo, the Islamic part of the city, with its segments of Roman walls and ancient structures. I just stood at the top and stared.

"Beautiful, isn't it?" asked the man standing beside me. He had dark hair and eyes and wasn't much older than I was. Obviously not a student or a student/tourist, he wore polished shoes and a sports coat. I recognized his Massachusetts accent.

"Not from around here, are you?" I asked. I'd heard that phrase on planes and boats throughout Egypt, as one English speaker greeted another.

"Not a very original thought," he said. And walked away.

Still only nine.

Dale came into the kitchen and glanced at the remains on the table. An empty wine bottle and glass, with dried pieces of cheese stuck to the plate. An ant was laboriously making his way across the dish to the cheese.

I scooped up the wine bottle and put it into the recycling bin. When I turned back for the glass and plate, Dale was putting them into the sink.

"Tough night?" he asked.

"My mom and I drank wine and ate cheese the night my dad died. I woke the next morning with a headache. Good news, no headache this time."

"You should have called me. You didn't need to drink wine alone. I could have sat here and talked about your mother with you. Or talked about your dad."

Dale had come to the house the afternoon my mother went to

make funeral arrangements for my dad. We'd spent the afternoon making out on my bed. I blushed at the memory.

"So, you remember that afternoon too?" asked Dale. "I felt so bad taking advantage of you when your dad died, but I'd wanted to kiss you for months. In perfect adolescent logic, that seemed like the day."

"And that led to all kinds of other things we shouldn't have done." I felt the need to change the subject.

"What are you doing these days?" I asked. "You seem to know everything about me, through my mother, and I know nothing about you."

"Yes, your mother is proud of you and your children. Even had some kind words for Magda, though I don't think she thinks much of him."

"Magda and my mother had differing views of the world," I said.

"But she let you marry him," said Dale.

I was not going there. Carol didn't approve of Magda any more than she did of Dale, back twenty years ago. But she let me make my own decision the second time around.

"I've read some of the books you wrote," I continued. "I like the detective you created, Blair Steele. But such a made-up name."

"All good detectives have made-up names." He smiled. It was a good smile. "It makes them memorable."

"So, how many books in the series? Five? Six?"

"Eight." He opened another bottle of wine and poured two generous glasses.

"Before we get into this bottle, did you talk to Richard?" I put out some more crackers and cheese.

"Yes, he suggested I contact Keene State in the morning and get information about your mother's health plan. Of course, we have information at home, but I need the out-of-state options. Richard says he has some information he'll bring to the meeting."

I didn't want to talk about my mother anymore. It wouldn't do any good, until we had more information, and it made me depressed.

"What do you do all day? Just sit at your computer and write?"

"God, no." He took a sip. "I can't live on what I make from writing. I have a job, twenty-five hours a week, at Citizen Advocacy."

"You mentioned that before. What is it you do there? Go to meetings with disabled people and make sure they get what they need?"

"Not exactly. We run a matchmaking service, without the sex. Just to match up friends and one of the friends has a disability."

"You're a matchmaker?" I reached for the crackers.

"Essentially. Citizen Advocacy was started by a man named Wolf Wolfsenberger in the 1970s. People were being released from state schools and institutions and placed in the community. Wolf's philosophy was that each person needed an advocate, a personal friend, who would help them negotiate the transition into the community. He thought that the advocates needed to be pillars of the community, so that the disabled person would be introduced to the church group, the Rotary, and other organizations."

"And you pay people to do this advocacy?"

Dale ignored his wine in his zeal to explain his job. "No, none of the advocates is paid. I get paid to do the match, but then the advocate and the disabled person control how their relationship is going to work. It's a powerful message when someone shows up to church, social security, or welfare or the clinic with a friend, rather than paid staff."

"How does that work?"

"Quite well, actually. We support dozens of relationships, some that have lasted for over twenty years. Funding sources sometimes have a problem, think that volunteers are unreliable, but we show them what we've done. We promote friendships that last."

I poured out the rest of the wine. "Is this how you got involved with my mother?"

"Not exactly. She knew about my work, and she's known me for almost thirty years, so she approached me when she realized she needed help. Or may need help."

"She'll need my help now." I picked up the wine bottle and stared at the label, willing the tears to go away. "After she gets out of rehab, I'll be taking her to live near me in Massachusetts."

Dale took the wine bottle from my hands. "How are you doing? Do you need help with something?"

"I'm scared about how my relationship with my mother will change. And whether I can take care of her, and how it's going to affect my family. Sometimes it seems overwhelming." Now I really was crying. Crying so hard I got the hiccups. I started searching through the cabinets for the tissues. I'd already gone through a box today.

Dale slid the box in front of me. It showed a moonlight scene, with trees and rabbits, white against the dark blue sky. Dumb scene for a tissue box.

Dale put his arm around me. I leaned against him and his shirt was soaked in a few minutes. He just held me and patted my back.

"It's not Carol I've loved all my life," he said. "It's you."

I backed away and sat down at the table. Picked at the crackers.

"Now you're hungry?" Dale started toward the pantry. "I think we need another bottle of wine." He came back out, holding a bottle of the raspberry merlot, and put it on the table.

I stood up. "Maybe another bottle of wine isn't a good idea."

"I think it's a great idea." Dale picked up the bottle and put his arm around my waist. "Now we need to go into the parlor for the entertainment."

"Parlor? I haven't heard anyone talk about a parlor in years. It's the family room, or the living room, or the great room."

"Your mother has a parlor." Dale led me into the room and we sat on the couch "Sit here, and we can share the wine."

"Share the wine and do what?" I'm not sure I wanted to do this.

"Watch TV. I got your mother a TV subscription service. It shows old movies and television shows."

"And what are we going to watch?"

He placed the wine glass in front of me. "*Highlander*," he said. "I remember the crush you had on Adrian Paul. Couldn't compete with a guy who lives forever."

I laughed. For the first time in days, I laughed. He was right, twenty years ago I had a serious crush on Adrian Paul. He played Duncan MacLeod, a four hundred-year-old immortal that went around fighting other immortals, righting wrongs, and bedding gorgeous women.

I didn't know whether wine was a good idea.

"How do you do it?" I asked.

"Do what?"

"Just keep going. I know you're concerned about Carol too, and you work with people with disabilities and you try to do stuff that is hard to do. Don't you get discouraged?"

"When I get discouraged, I think of you." Dale placed the wine on the table.

I stared at the bottle, so I wouldn't have to look at Dale. "You think of me?"

"Yes, you're one of the best things that has happened in my life. You and Heather." He took my hands again. "When I write about true love and lasting relationships, I think of you. When I help people with disabilities, especially children, I think I'm giving something back to the world for my decision about Heather." Dale produced a corkscrew from somewhere, and opened the bottle. "Do you want more wine?"

"Sure."

Dale put his arm around me. "We hardly talked after you left for Europe and the Middle East. I've missed you."

"I got married. I moved on."

"I know."

"And you never contacted me." I was crying again.

"I didn't know you wanted me to."

"Don't you understand? There's a twenty-year gap. I don't know anything about you."

"What do you want to know?"

"Everything. What did you do after I left?"

"I started writing. Been writing for twenty years. Got some rabid fans and some people who don't care for my books. Anything else you want to know?"

So many things. He obviously still thought of me and Heather. Did he have a plan for finding Heather or was it just a hope? What did he talk about with my mother? What did he do all day? Did he still lay around all day in his pajama bottoms? Don't go there. I didn't need to think about him lying around all day in just his pajama bottoms. Or nothing at all. I shook my head.

"Why are you shaking your head? Don't you believe me?"

"I believe you," I said.

"Shall we move on to the entertainment portion of the evening?"

"Entertainment?" Again, that image of him in just his pajama bottoms.

"Yes, the *Highlander* part."

We watched several episodes of Duncan MacLeod vanquishing other immortals and saving the world. Somewhere between the second and third episodes, Dale kissed me. The first one was just a peck but the second one went on forever.

"That's something I've wanted to do for a long time," said Dale.

"What happens next?" I was truly curious, because I couldn't think about even the next half hour.

"We've both had too much to drink to make a rational decision." Dale stood up. "So you're going up to bed and I'm going to my room."

I was surprised at my disappointment. I had unfinished business with Dale. I needed to decide how we were going to interact in the future. If I moved my mother to Massachusetts, he would be homeless. He was a decent caretaker, would he come with her to continue to care for her? What would Magda say if Dale were around on a daily basis? Right now, Dale was loving and kind and helpful. Magda was far away and complaining. I didn't want to make that decision now.

TUESDAY

I WOKE UP ALONE IN MY BED. I SMELLED COFFEE, THOUGH IT was still dark outside. 4:20 a.m. I'd been asleep over four hours and the effects of the alcohol were wearing off. All that was left was the gritty taste in my mouth.

I was cold. I had thrown off the covers while I slept. I wanted coffee, but first I needed to get the foul taste out of my mouth. I went into the bathroom, brushed my teeth, and felt almost human.

I went downstairs and into the kitchen. Dale was pouring himself a cup.

"What are you doing up at this time of night?"

Dale turned toward me. "Drinking coffee. I couldn't sleep."

I sat down at the table. Dale put the cup down in front of me. The mingling of toothpaste and coffee was sharp but not unpleasant.

"Can I help?" Dale asked.

I wanted to cry but found I had no tears left. I was a mother and a judge. I needed to stop crying. "I don't think there's anything you can do."

"That's the rub, isn't it?" Dale took a sip of his coffee. "I can't do anything for you. And I haven't done anything for you."

I felt like I had missed part of this conversation. Dale looked so miserable. "What do you mean?" I was genuinely confused.

"I didn't stick around when you had our daughter. And I stayed away for twenty years, even though I missed you every day." He reached out and took my hand. "And now you've got a life I'm not part of and you don't want my help to find Heather."

His thumb stroked the outside of my hand. "Dale, I've moved on. I made my decisions and I live with them. I have three children to think of. Four, if you count Heather. And I do."

"But don't you want to remember sometimes?" He got up, came around the table, and lifted me up by the elbows.

Not a real lift. I came willingly. And he kissed me again.

"Let's remember, just for one night," he said.

I followed him up the stairs.

Dale had taken all the covers during the night. I didn't remember this from our previous relationship. But then, we were young and seldom spent the entire night together. I pulled the covers over to my side and Dale came with them. He was very warm and very big and took up a lot of space in the bed. So unlike Magda, who was polite and discrete, even while asleep.

Magda. I hadn't even though about Magda last night, or early this morning, or whenever I decided I needed to connect with Dale. Just thought about being with Dale, having to make decisions for my mother, and not knowing what happened to Heather.

Dale was staring at me. "Any regrets?" he asked.

Dale was a huge part of my past and we had created a child together. He did matter. But I knew nothing about him for the last twenty years. I'm so confused.

Dale propped himself on one elbow and stared down at me.

"I have a list of regrets," I said. None that I wanted to share with him.

He rolled over and stood up, his back to me. Even his back looked good. A scar on the back of his knee and one on his shoulder made him look like he'd done some living. He didn't have those scars twenty years ago.

He pulled on his jeans and left the room.

What the hell was I going to do now? I'd made a dumb mistake, and not my first with Dale. I couldn't go back twenty years, no matter how much I wanted to. And I didn't want to forget the three children who lived with me.

My phone buzzed. Magda. I ignored it. Then I got a text from him: *Please call. It's important.* I pushed the buttons and he picked up immediately.

"Did I wake you up?" Magda asked.

"No, I was up. Just in the bathroom. What's so important?"

"The Assistant DA has agreed to dismiss the charges against Ash. Hearing is set for Thursday morning. I think we need to get this over."

"Agreed." I would have to move cases, again, but Ash needed me. "I'll be there. Is there anything they need from us before the court date?"

"He didn't mention anything, but I'll ask specifically. Get back to you on that." I heard the scratch of a pen on paper; Magda still kept a paper calendar. "How are things going there?"

"Slowly," I said. "We are supposed to have a treatment meeting this morning and I'll know more afterward. We need to talk about moving my mother to Massachusetts if she needs daily help."

"I'll do some research online." I heard the pen scratching again. "See what's available here. I think she'd have more options in Massachusetts than in New Hampshire. Does Dale come with her?"

"That's one of the things we need to talk about." But not now. "I've got to go. Love you."

"Ditto." And Magda was gone.

I walked down the stairs slowly, knowing I would have to confront another problem at the bottom.

Dale was making breakfast. Eggs and bacon. "Thought I'd make us something to eat. No telling how long we'll be at the hospital, meeting with people."

"That's good." I sat down. "I just talked to Magda."

"Oh?" He placed a plate in front of me.

"I'm staying with Magda."

Dale sat down across from me. "I thought you would."

"You did?" This might be easier than I thought.

"Last night, I thought we needed to connect like we used to. Today, I realize you have moved on. You have a husband, children, a career you're good at. I don't have a place in that."

"You're taking care of my mother. That's a big thing."

"And if she goes to assisted living or elderly housing? Do you expect me to go with her?"

I picked at my food. "I hadn't thought that far. Though Magda did say he may not want you around if my mother moved to Massachusetts."

"Of course he doesn't." Dale started eating.

I sat down at my computer and sent a text to the courthouse, letting them know I'll be in late today. Then I called the courthouse and left a message, saying essentially the same thing. I didn't want to talk to anyone and they needed an early notice anyway, so 8:00 a.m. seemed an appropriate time to do the notifications.

Twenty-two texts from the kids. Pamela had nothing to wear and neither Magda nor Ashroff was willing to take her shopping. I sent her a note, saying she was grounded and shouldn't be out shopping anyway. Phillip, my sensitive one, said he missed me and he wanted to know how Grandma was doing. Ashroff commented on his "out of control" father. He also wanted to make sure that I knew his final exams started in a week and he needed to be there.

Dale wandered into the den as I finished. A fly buzzed against the window.

"I miss her too," Dale said. "I miss her every day."

I felt the wetness on my cheeks again. "I don't know why I'm crying about something that happened over twenty years ago."

"I do." Dale sat across from me and entwined his fingers with mine. "Grief is cumulative. Your mother almost died, and you think about what else you lost."

"I try not to think of her as lost," I said. "I like to think of her as growing up in a huge white house with loving parents."

"But don't you want to know?" he asked.

"Right now, I want to concentrate on my mother. We need to get to the hospital and see what's going on."

Dale picked up his keys. "I'll drive."

"I'm taking my car too. I don't know what we'll need to do after we meet with the doctor and the physical therapist."

Richard was already at Cheshire Medical Center when we arrived. He was on his scooter and still had his jacket on.

"Good morning," Richard said. "I brought some information you may want to read. It's in my backpack." An L.L. Bean backpack hung from the back of his scooter. "Where is this meeting?"

I pulled the notice from my purse. "It says Conference Room 133. Wherever that is."

"This way." Richard gestured with his left arm. He did seem to know his way around the facility.

We found the room with no problem. It was small, with a table and half a dozen chairs. And warm. Dale and I took off our jackets. Richard struggled with his. I reached over to help him get the jacket off his right arm.

He grimaced and gave an involuntary "Oh."

"Are you hurt?" I asked.

"Please don't assume I need help," Richard said. "If I need help, I'll ask for it." He took off the jacket with another grimace. "Or you can ask me if I need help."

"I'm sorry, I didn't know." I felt foolish at assuming he couldn't do something he probably did on a daily basis. But that didn't stop me from asking the obvious question. "Are you injured? Your arm seems to hurt and you still have the remains of a black eye." The eye I'd noticed in the park had faded to a dull yellow.

"I'm clumsy, I fall off my scooter and get bruised." He held out his coat. "Would you please hang this up?"

I put his coat, and mine, on the coatrack in the corner. Dale put his coat on the back of a chair.

"Wasn't this meeting called for ten thirty?" Dale asked.

The clock on the wall said 10:42.

The door opened and a woman, dressed in maroon scrubs, came into the room. "I'm Elizabeth Hanley, the radiologist." She shook hands with each of us.

"I don't have much to tell you." Ms. Hanley sat down at the table. "We are taking new images, because of the stroke Mrs. Donnelly suffered yesterday. Her femur is healing as we expected and there are beds available in the area. But Dr. Josefson cannot release your mother until we get more information."

"Ms. Hanley—" I started.

"It's Dr. Hanley."

"Dr. Hanley, what exactly are you doing about my mother?"

"We are taking new images. An echocardiogram and other tests that will give us more information about her condition and what steps we need to take next."

"Where are the other doctors? Dr. Josefson? The physical therapist?"

"They should be here shortly. I've got to go now, to do further testing." Dr. Hanley left the room.

Richard moved his scooter closer to the table. "While we're waiting, I can let you know what I found about your mother's insurance and care. Would you please get my backpack and put it on the table?"

Dale put the backpack in front of him. Richard took the documents out and placed them in three piles in front of him.

Richard looked at me. "Your mother has very good insurance. It will cover her in all the New England states. I've divided the information into three piles. Short-term orthopedic rehab, long-term care at home, either in New Hampshire or Massachusetts, and long-term care in a facility. I'd have added short-term cardiac rehab, but that's a new development."

Richard went into the intricacies of insurance and long-term care. I felt my eyes glazing over.

Richard stopped talking for several seconds. "I know it's a lot. And we can't make any definitive decisions until we know what the plan is. I've made copies of everything, so you can take it home and study it."

Dale put his hand on my arm. "It's okay, Abbi, we'll figure it out?"

I looked over at him. Remembered all that we shared.

"Are the two of you going to take care of Mrs. Donnelly? Don't you live in Massachusetts with your husband?"

My husband. I needed to be more careful how I looked at Dale.

The morning was a marathon of waiting, punctuated by meetings in which nobody made a conclusive statement. When the nurse had talked about planning for my mother, I pictured a huge table, with everyone sitting around it, and making a comprehensive plan for what was going to happen and when. The doctor was running more tests. The radiologist needed to read the images, or ultrasound, or whatever the images were. The physical therapist couldn't assess my mother until she woke up and was more responsive.

For years, I'd heard complaints about the legal system, and the people involved in it waiting around for something to happen. I'd brushed it off as a symptom of a deliberative system. I didn't like being on the other side of the table, trying to figure out what was happening.

Dale, Richard, and I went to visit my mother. Her room was empty and we were told that she was still undergoing tests and imaging.

"I'm going back to Massachusetts." Richard and Dale were the only people in my mother's room when I made this statement.

"When?"

"Now." I tried to sound in charge. "Nobody here can tell me what's going on and probably won't have answers for hours. I'll go check on my children, and my courtroom, and then I'll come back to Keene tonight. It's only about an hour, some people do that as a commute every day."

Dale opened and closed his mouth. "Let's go back to the conference room. Maybe we'll have more information now."

I gave a noncommittal shrug and we all went back to the conference room to find Dr. Josefson there. "I'm sorry this morning has been so chaotic. When we scheduled this meeting, we assumed we would have all the information we needed to make a plan. Because of the stroke, we're still running tests and getting results." She put a stack of files on the table, her laptop perched at the summit.

"Can you come back tomorrow morning? We should have more information and can make a plan then."

I opened my mouth to let her know that I was a judge and had other things to do. But none more important. Dale and I nodded our assent. Richard had a meeting in Meredith, but we had his information and would reach him later in the day.

"Can we move the meeting up, to earlier in the morning?" I asked.

"I'm here at seven," said Dr. Josefson. "But you may want to give us some time to get things together before the meeting. How about nine?"

I rearranged things in my head and agreed.

I spent the drive to Massachusetts wondering if I'd make a mistake. What if my mother had another stroke? That's probably the only emergency situation, and she was in a hospital. If they needed to run more tests, or make arrangements for care after she left the hospital, that wouldn't happen suddenly. And I needed to see what was going on with my family. I would stop at the court and pick up files that needed written decisions. I'd have to make copies of the relevant documents, as I can't take the originals from the courthouse, but that would allow me to write while I was waiting at the hospital. I'd take care of the cases assigned to me today, then I'd go home and check on the kids when they got back from school. If I left for Keene by six, I could check in on my mother before the end of visiting hours. Not a great plan, but a plan.

I parked the car and took the back stairs to the judge's lobby. I didn't feel like having multiple conversations about my mother, but the information transfer in the courthouse is almost instantaneous. I wasn't in my office more than ten minutes when Cally knocked at my door. He had a newspaper in his hand.

"Cally, what's on for this afternoon? I'm hoping I can be back in Keene this evening to see my mother."

Cally sat down in the chair in my office. "How are you doing?"

"About as well as can be expected."

"I heard about your mother." Cally placed the newspaper on my desk. "I'm sorry. It must be hard to deal with."

"I'm managing," I said. "What's with the newspaper?"

"There's a whole article in that about Attorney Paoletti." Cally flipped the paper open. "Good thing we had the going away party before this came out."

"What came out?" I picked up the paper. "I've been in New Hampshire and haven't heard the local news."

I looked at the headline: *Local Attorney Father of Murdered Woman's Child.*

I read on: "Gerard Paoletti is the father of the child carried by Jenna Jay, who was murdered last Wednesday. This according to Kendra Jenkins, the District Attorney, who held a press conference this morning. Jenna Jay, a clerk in the Juvenile Court, was found murdered in the courthouse. She was found to be pregnant and, after testing, Gerard Paoletti, a local attorney, was determined to be the father. Attorney Paoletti is now a person of interest in the homicide."

The article went on but I stopped reading.

"What does this mean?" I asked.

"It means that Gerard was bonking Jenna," said Cally. "And he's in a mess of trouble."

"No, I can't believe that. Jenna and Chloe were happy together."

"You never can tell what goes on in a marriage." Cally picked up the paper. "Do you need a few minutes before we start?"

He dropped the bombshell about Jenna on me and then asked if I needed a few minutes. Maybe he meant to get ready for court. Either way, I'd take him up on it. "Give me fifteen minutes, then come back to get me for the afternoon session."

I should call Chloe and ask her what's going on. She told me that Jenna was pregnant from a surrogate and that they planned the pregnancy. She was adamant and definite that it involved "some technology."

But first I had to get through the afternoon's cases.

I had been assigned the matter of George Banks. He made the headlines in a local paper a few months ago when he got into the courthouse with a pistol and threatened Judge Ramos. Judge Ramos couldn't hear the case, for obvious reasons, and the other justice in Worcester had done the original adoption petition. So, the tangled mess ended up in my courtroom.

In my lobby with me were Albert Montoya, attorney for Mr. Banks, and the Department of Children and Families (DCF) attorney, Evan Hunter. The regular DCF attorney, Niagara Fontaine, had been removed from the case because of some contact with Mr. Banks. Also present was Attorney Warner; she represented that the child wanted to stay with her adoptive parents.

I went through the pile of paperwork on my desk. The file was three inches thick and I had reviewed it the night before. Now I wanted to know what the attorneys had to say.

"Attorney Hunter, what is the Department's position in this matter?"

Attorney Hunter opened the file on his lap. This was a

high-profile case; I was reasonably sure he already knew the facts.

"As you know, Judge Hartwell," Hunter began. "George Banks had his parental rights terminated in this court because of his incarceration. He had not parented his child or lived with the child's mother during any of her life. The child, a girl, Charity, has been adopted and has lived with her forever family for over four years. She is enrolled in kindergarten and is doing well with her new family."

"All that may be true," said Montoya. "But we are here about George Banks and his motion to reopen the proceedings. His conviction has been overturned and his incarceration was the reason for losing his child. As the incarceration was illegal, so is the termination based upon the incarceration."

"It's not like the defendant was exonerated because he could not have done the crime," Hunter responded. "His conviction was overturned because of wrongdoing by a state chemist. I have the newspaper articles here." Hunter put another stack of papers on my desk.

I went through the articles, though I knew the facts. A second reason the case was high profile was because a chemist in the Massachusetts state laboratory had been discharged because of drug use on the job; this fact was substantiated by a series of her drug screens that were positive for methamphetamines, opioids, and benzodiazepines. After her discharge, it was determined that she had been falsifying the results of drug tests over a period of years and, in some cases, took the confiscated drugs she was supposed to be testing. After a lengthy investigation, and prolonged negotiations between the Attorney General, the county District Attorneys, and the defense bar, over two thousand convictions were overturned or called into question because of the actions of the dismissed chemist.

"George Banks had been convicted of possession of cocaine and, as the amount was large, possession with intent to distribute,"

Hunter continued. "He pled guilty and was sentenced to four years, a lesser sentence than he would receive had he gone to trial. He knew the substance was cocaine and he knew the Commonwealth could prove that he was distributing it."

"But the Commonwealth couldn't prove it," interrupted Montoya. "The tests were faulty, the chemist was charged and found guilty of eight counts of fraud. She's now in jail. Without the tainted evidence, my client would be with his child now."

"That seems unlikely." Hunter shut the file on his lap. "Mr. Banks has a history of arrests and even he believed the test would come back positive for cocaine. Charity's adoption is final, Mr. Banks was given adequate notice, and there is no legal basis for voiding the adoption at this time."

"Attorney Warner, what is your position?" I asked.

"The child wants to stay with her adoptive parents, where she has resided for four years." Attorney Warner laid a picture on my desk. "This is my client, in her kindergarten picture. She does not know her father and is happy in her present home."

"As your client is only five years old, I am presuming that you are substituting your judgment for hers." I asked the same question every time.

"I am." Warner had the grace to acknowledge her words were not the words of the child. "But I did talk to my client and she considers her adoptive parent her mother. She does not remember Mr. Banks."

A knock sounded at the door. I looked through the panel on the side of the door and saw Cally, the court officer, standing and waiting for me. I stood and opened the door

"Judge Hartwell, we're ready for you in Courtroom Two," he said. "Presiding judge assigned you a few matters before you start the hearing on Mr. Banks." Cally stood with his hands on his belt. He had been sent to diplomatically tell me to get moving. He'd delivered the message, but didn't want me to think he had a stake in the outcome.

"Yes, I understand that everyone's waiting for me." I stepped back into the room. "Tell them I'll be out in ten minutes."

"Judge, adoptions have been overturned in the past." Attorney Montoya picked up his argument where it left off. "The Baby M case, other cases where the father did not get a fair shake."

"Those cases had one thing in common. The father was not notified." Attorney Hunter waved his hands to the left, as if he were pushing away that argument. "This father was notified and failed to appear in court. The adoption should remain final."

"Okay, let's bottom line this." I sat down at the table, across from the attorneys. "Mr. Banks has a substance abuse problem and past criminal convictions, even before the case that got him incarcerated. The child has been adopted and is doing well in her new home. Is there any arrangement we can make to allow Mr. Banks to take a part in his biological daughter's life?"

"The adoptive parent does not want to deal with Mr. Banks and his substance abuse issues. I have a letter from her, discussing Charity's gains and her concerns." Hunter pulled a letter, written on actual stationary with a letterhead, from his file.

I looked at him and at the letter. Didn't take it from him. He put it on the table.

"Attorney Hunter, you and I know that the adoptive parent has a right to be heard." I put my hand on the letter. "But this isn't the time or the place. How about visits at a visitation center? Would the adoptive parent agree to that?"

"It may address some of her concerns." Hunter wasn't giving in.

"My client would not agree to that," said Montoya. "If he is a fit parent, and he has been sober for two years, then he should have unsupervised visits."

Montoya needed a reality check.

"You know you have a high hurdle to overturn a finalized adoption," I said.

"I think all of us can agree that these circumstances are unique."

Montoya did have a point. But I had another one. "Mr. Banks now faces additional charges for bringing a firearm into the courthouse. He may be in jail and unavailable anyway."

"To say the least, he was under extreme emotional duress." Attorney Montoya started packing up his briefcase. "But that argument is for another day. Today, I just want my motion to reopen the case to be heard."

We all exited my office. Cally still stood in the corridor and escorted us all into the courtroom. I quickly disposed of the other matters I had been assigned.

The attorneys on the Banks case entered the courtroom. Each of them made an opening statement, summarizing what I had learned in the judge's lobby. Attorney Montoya, for George Banks, wanted the termination of parental rights and the adoption voided, so that the proceedings would start again. Attorney Hunter, for the Department, wanted the motion denied and the adoption to stand. Attorney Warner, for the child, argued that remaining in her present home was in the child's best interests.

As it was Attorney Montoya's motion, he went first. The parties had agreed to enter documents as evidence of the criminal case and its dismissal. Attorney Montoya started by entering into evidence the docket on Mr. Banks's case, the docket on the chemist's case, the findings in the previous adoption petition, and a four-page list of stipulations of the parties. All this had been marked and entered, and it cut down on the testimony.

George Banks looked good. He had been in yet another substance abuse treatment program and appeared to have benefited from it. He was neatly dressed in a suit but no tie, his hair was recently cut, and he appeared clear-eyed and ready to proceed.

The hearing started with Mr. Banks's substance abuse counselor, Alicia Bushey. She testified that Mr. Banks came to the clinic every week for his suboxone treatment. She went into a detailed, geeky explanation of how suboxone inhibited the cravings for heroin and opioids while lessening the chance of an overdose, should the subject use again. And then a clinical explanation about how substance abuse was a medical concern, not a legal one, and how relapse and setbacks were part of the process. I'd heard all this before and the parties could have stipulated to that testimony. Nobody ever did, because they wanted me to hear it every time. Much more interesting were the specifics of Mr. Banks's treatment.

"How long have you been treating Mr. Banks?" asked Attorney Montoya.

"Ten months."

"Please describe his specific treatment plan."

"George comes in to the clinic on a weekly basis to get his suboxone. He only gets one month's prescription at a time, and he is required to come in to the clinic every week to pick up seven days' worth of suboxone. He sees me for counseling, also on a weekly basis, and is randomly drug tested. Every six months, he sees a physician at the clinic to be reevaluated."

Ms. Bushey only answered the question, then stopped. She was either experienced at testifying or well prepped by Attorney Montoya.

"What do you and Mr. Banks work on in counseling?" asked Attorney Montoya.

'We work on daily living skills. How to cope with cravings, how to get and keep a job, how to deal with negative comments from the public."

"Do you do what is considered traditional therapy? Talk about his past, trying to work through any mental health issues?"

"George has a long-term therapist for his mental health issues. I deal with his substance abuse issues." Ms. Bushey shifted in her chair and looked around the room. "He's working very hard at remaining sober and putting his life together. He needs to see his child."

Maybe Ms. Bushey wasn't as well prepared as she seemed. That was definitely off script. Attorney Montoya ignored her statements about Mr. Banks's motivation.

"Does Mr. Banks talk to you about his sessions with his therapist?"

Attorney Montoya was walking a fine line here. Conversations with a therapist were generally privileged, but not if Mr. Banks's attorney entered them into evidence.

"His therapist sent me a letter saying Mr. Banks suffered from ADHD; that's Attention Deficit Hyperactivity Disorder. And, after his release from jail, PTSD, which is Post Traumatic Stress Disorder. His therapist gave me some worksheets and tips for working with Mr. Banks, but I have not discussed anything Mr. Banks told his therapist."

We were back to the well-rehearsed witness. She knew just what to say to avoid Mr. Banks's statements to his therapist coming into trial. Or maybe I was just cynical and jaded. Maybe Mr. Banks was a good guy who got a bad deal. But he had a history of criminal involvement even before his most recent incarceration. Attorney Hunter's cross-examination went directly to that point.

"Ms. Bushey, do you know why Mr. Banks was in jail?" Attorney Hunter always started with the big questions.

"He was falsely accused of possession of cocaine." Ms. Bushey looked around the room again.

"How do you know he was falsely accused?" asked Hunter.

"That's why we're here, isn't it? Because the state screwed up and you can't prove that he had cocaine." Ms. Bushey crossed her arms across her chest.

"Mr. Banks pled guilty to possession of cocaine, did he not?"

"I don't know."

"You don't know whether Mr. Banks pled guilty to possession of cocaine?"

"That's what I said." Ms. Bushey turned to me. "Your Honor, could I have a drink of water please?"

There were water carafes on the attorneys' tables, but the proceedings were interrupted while water was poured and taken to the witness. She took tiny sips.

"Are you ready to resume?" I asked. Both Attorney Hunter and Ms. Bushy indicated that they were.

Attorney Hunter asked another question. "Ms. Bushey, have you seen Mr. Banks's criminal record?"

"A while ago." Ms. Bushey balanced the water glass on the ledge before her. The court officer came and took it away. "I don't remember everything in it."

"But you do remember he is falsely accused of possession of cocaine."

"Yes, that's what he told me in group." Ms. Bushey looked at Mr. Banks.

"In group?"

"Yes, in addition to seeing me every week, Mr. Banks attends our 'here and now' group."

"What is a 'here and now' group?" Attorney Hunter seemed genuinely interested.

"It's a group where we discuss issues faced by people with a substance abuse history or criminal charges because of substance abuse."

"But substance abuse is not a crime."

"Of course not." Ms. Bushey put her arms across her chest again. "But there is a stigma in this society against people with those issues."

"And what did Mr. Banks say about his past substance abuse and his past criminal charges?"

"He said they were exaggerated and taken out of context," Bushey replied. "He admits to having a problem, but he is seeking treatment and he has always held down a job."

"How many times has Mr. Banks been convicted of possession of cocaine or possession of heroin?"

"A few."

"Seven times, Ms. Bushey, he has been convicted seven times in the last twelve years." Attorney Hunter flipped through his file. "And how many times has Mr. Banks been arrested for possession with intent to sell cocaine or heroin?"

"Those charges were dismissed." Ms. Bushey barely waited for Attorney Hunter to finish.

"Three times he was arrested, two charges were dismissed."

"He told me about that. He said the cops were always after him. We talked about this in group. Once the cops arrest you once, they are all over you looking for any minor thing you do wrong."

Attorney Hunter, knowing the significance of her answer, stood by the table for a few minutes to let me absorb what she said.

My estimation of Ms. Bushey as a witness was going down fast. With that last answer, she sounded like Mr. Banks's advocate, not an expert witness on substance abuse treatment.

"But you agree that Mr. Banks has a substance abuse problem?" Attorney Hunter asked.

"Yes."

"And how does that substance abuse problem impact his parenting?"

"I don't know." Ms. Bushey had picked up her pen and was spinning it between her fingers. "It has deprived him of the right to parent."

"You would agree that incarceration would also impact Mr. Banks's ability to parent?"

The silence was prolonged. I wondered if Ms. Bushey didn't understand the question. She finally answered.

"It has already impacted his parenting. He could not object to the termination of his parental rights, so they were taken away. He only wants a level playing field."

"Ms. Bushey, you are aware that Mr. Banks is facing new criminal charges from an incident last fall?" Hunter picked up another file. "He is being charged with illegal possession of a firearm and with intimidating a witness in that matter."

"He was set up. His lawyer brought the gun into the courthouse, he didn't. She talked him into using it to get his kids back." Ms. Bushey's face was red. "He got really, really bad legal advice and he shouldn't be punished for it. She should."

Ms. Bushey had clearly crossed the line to actively advocating for Mr. Banks. She wasn't testifying about his treatment or his prognosis for recovery, she was taking his side in a legal dispute.

"Objection, Your Honor." Attorney Montoya was on his feet. "Motion to strike the answer as non-responsive."

"Attorney Montoya," I said. "This is your witness. Mr. Hunter can ask her about her biases. You qualified her as an expert, so he can ask about her opinion. What is your objection?"

Before he could answer, Ms. Bushey spoke again. "There is nothing objectionable in what I said. The legal system, and his attorney, are out to get George Banks." Her face was even redder during this speech.

"It's 12:30. Let's break for lunch. Everyone can get something to eat and calm down. We will resume at 1:45."

I left the bench before I lost my temper. Maybe I had reacted more as a mother than a judge. But everyone was getting unreasonable. Eating and thinking about what they wanted to say couldn't hurt.

George Banks testified after lunch.

"Mr. Banks, are you the father of Charity?"

"Yes, sir,"

"And you were married to Charity's mother when she was born?"

"Yes, sir. My name is on the birth certificate."

"And were you living with Charity's mother when she was born?"

"Yes, sir."

Attorney Montoya was clearly leading his client but Attorney Hunter didn't object. He wanted to get the preliminaries over.

"When was the last time you saw Charity?"

"The day they arrested me on the bogus charge. She was three months old."

"And you were notified about the custody proceeding in this court?"

"They sent me a certified letter. Not much I could do about it in jail."

"And what happened to the charges that you were arrested on when Charity was three months old?"

"They were dismissed. All of them."

"And you were released from jail?"

"Yeah, last August. Then I got arrested and went back to jail in November."

"And then you were released again? On a monitoring bracelet?"

"Yeah, I have to pay every month for the bracelet and to see probation. I got to pay."

Attorney Montoya shuffled papers while Mr. Banks took a deep breath. Attorney Montoya took him through his substance abuse treatment, as outlined by Ms. Bushey. Mr. Banks had also developed a relapse prevention plan and had started a parenting class. Mr. Banks did well, better than Ms. Bushey. He stayed calm and focused.

Attorney Montoya finished his direct examination and Attorney Hunter stood up.

He started right in on Mr. Banks.

"Mr. Banks, did you bring a gun into the courthouse in November of last year?"

Attorney Montoya was on his feet. "Your Honor, my client asserts his Fifth Amendment rights."

"Mr. Banks, did you possess a firearm without a license in November of last year?"

"Fifth Amendment."

"Did you threaten the court clerk Priscilla Hayden with a

firearm in November of last year?"

"Fifth Amendment."

Attorney Hunter threw down his pen in mock indignation. I'd seen that move before.

Hunter addressed the court. "Your Honor, I ask that the court draw a negative inference from each question that Mr. Banks refused to answer."

Montoya was on his feet. "Your Honor, my client has all the Fifth Amendment rights allowed to any U.S. citizen. He has a criminal trial pending and, on advice of both his criminal and his juvenile attorneys, will not testify to matters covered in his criminal matter. Drawing a negative inference would put him at a disadvantage."

"Counsel, I've heard these arguments before." I looked over the bench at both attorneys. They knew what I was going to say next, but I needed to say it for the benefit of Mr. Banks and anyone else in the courtroom who didn't know the law. "In a criminal case, Mr. Banks has an absolute right against self-incrimination. He is presumed not guilty and he cannot be forced to testify. Neither a judge nor a jury can penalize him or find him guilty because of his failure to testify." I shuffled some papers on my desk, because I wanted everyone to think about what I said. The system didn't always work that way, but that was the standard.

I continued on. "But this is a civil matter. The standard is not 'beyond a reasonable doubt' but 'clear and convincing evidence.' I cannot send Mr. Banks to jail for what he has done or not done in the past. However, because he doesn't face incarceration, he does not have an absolute right against self-incrimination. If he refused to testify, I can draw what is called a 'negative inference,' or I can determine that he is not testifying because the testimony would be harmful to his case. It's totally within my discretion. But, because the charges facing Mr. Banks are so serious, I am not going to draw a negative inference against him."

Hunter jumped to his feet. Montoya rose more slowly and asked if he could discuss this matter with his client. I ordered a fifteen-minute recess. Went and hid in my office.

There were two pink slips on my desk. Nobody got to talk directly to the judge, so my messages were screened and the court still used pink slips. One was about rescheduling a case. That could wait. The other was from Dennis Raymond, the person Jenna called before she died. He didn't know if he could be helpful but was willing to meet with me at five thirty today. I called and left a message on his voicemail, confirming the appointment.

Cally escorted me back into the courtroom. The attorneys continued their arguments. Most of the Commonwealth's case was documents: documents notifying George Banks of the proceeding, documents of incarceration, documents terminating his parental rights.

The case would come down to George Banks, his credibility, and his situation. I took the entire matter under advisement and dismissed the attorneys and their clients.

At five thirty, I was standing outside the Ascend office. Though it was after regular office hours, the place was full of people. People wandered in and out, speaking at least three different languages. I asked for Dennis Raymond.

I was escorted to a tiny office, probably ten feet by eight feet. Stuffed into it were a metal desk, two chairs, a file cabinet and dozens of paper files. A computer and printer took up most of the space on the desktop.

Mr. Raymond sat behind the desk and gestured me toward the other chair. "We don't get many judges in this office," he said.

"It's not often that my clerk is killed."

"There is that." He moved a stack of files from one side of the desk to the other. "You know that our work here is confidential."

"Look, Mr. Raymond, I could have just called," I slid forward in the wooden seat, "but I wanted to talk to you face-to-face. You were the last person Jenna called before she died. It wasn't court related, or I would have known about it. What did you talk about?"

"As I said, our work is confidential. As it wasn't part of her job, I can't talk about it."

"You can't talk about what she said." I was an expert on privilege. "So, let's talk about how she appeared, what she felt."

Raymond stared out of the tiny window, as if looking for answers. "She was scared."

"Scared of what? Did you tell the police?"

"The police haven't been to see me," Raymond said. "When they called, I led them to believe the call was part of her job."

"It wasn't." I said it as a statement, not a question. "What was she scared of?"

"She wasn't specific. But she wanted to enter our protected domestic violence system."

Raymond really seemed to want to talk, so I remained silent until he went on.

"She did say that she wanted to get away from someone and they couldn't know where she was."

"Did she tell you she was married?"

"She did. Really, I can't tell you much. She left before we finished our conversation."

"Why?" I asked. "Did she get a phone call, see someone?"

"No, she just said she remembered another appointment and needed to leave. We made another time to meet the next day. And, of course, she never returned."

"What about the phone call on the day she died?"

"She left a message on my voicemail that she wanted to talk to me," said Raymond. "That's what I told the police."

I knew I wasn't getting any more from Raymond.

I walked back through the crowded lobby. It looked like even more people had arrived in the short time I was with Raymond. I stood in the parking lot. So much was going on with Jenna that I didn't know about. She and Chloe seemed so happy. Had I been that blind to what was going on?

I wasn't going to call Chloe. I'd be better if I just showed up at her door. It looked like I wouldn't get back to see my mother tonight. I texted Dale to tell him that and to affirm that I'd be at the meeting in the morning.

As my father used to say, Chloe looked like she'd been rode hard and put away wet. I think the reference was to horses, but Chloe looked like hell.

She stood in the doorway and stared at me.

"May I come in?" I asked.

She stood back and made a gesture I interpreted as assent. We went into the side room and sat down. No offer of food or drink.

"I guess you've seen the paper," Chloe said.

"I have."

"It wasn't supposed to come out this way." Chloe stood up, put her arms around her torso, and walked to the window. "Jenna would be so embarrassed."

"I think Jenna is beyond embarrassment."

"I know, but it still hurts." Chloe started crying.

I looked around the room. No tissue box to mar the exact placement of everything in the room. I pulled a bunch of clean tissue from my purse, walked over and gave them to Chloe.

I heard the click of toenails and Max came into the room.

"Oh, Max." Chloe pressed the tissue to her eyes. "I forgot to feed Max."

Chloe started down the hallway to her kitchen and I followed her. I stood in the doorway as she got out a can of dog food, put it into a silver bowl, and added dry dog food to the top. She put it on the floor and Max gobbled it down.

"Poor baby, you've been neglected with Jenna gone." Chloe knelt next to Max.

"Chloe," I said.

She stood up. "I've got to walk Max. After he eats, he needs to be walked." She went to the coat closet and took out a light jacket and a leash.

"I'll come with you," I said. It meant Chloe would be looking at Max, not me, but I wasn't fussy about how I got the information.

"Oh, okay." She put on her coat. It took a few moments to get the leash on Max, who was prancing around the kitchen. "We may be gone for a while. You may want to come back and talk to me later."

"No, Chloe, I don't want to come back. I'm going with you."

She gave a shrug and opened the door. Max, after the initial prancing, was well behaved and walked at our side. We got as far as the end of the driveway.

A woman walked up to us. "Are you Chloe Jay?"

"No, I'm not." Chloe attempted to get Max past her.

Max wasn't cooperating. He kept sniffing her red, high-heeled shoes. Chloe pulled on the leash.

"Yes, you are. I'm Melody Tan from WWRP. Would you be willing to do an interview?"

"No." Chloe grabbed hold of Max's collar and pulled him to her side.

Melody turned to me. "And who are you? Are you involved in Jenna Jay's murder?"

"No comment." I was glad she wasn't the courthouse reporter or she would've recognized me.

Chloe dragged Max back up the driveway. Melody followed.

"If you want to give a statement, I can assure you that it will run on the news tonight." Melody stuck her microphone in front of Chloe.

Chloe climbed the steps of the front porch and stopped. If she was going to give a statement, I wasn't going to be part of it. I opened the door.

"You're trespassing. Please get off me property." Chloe took Max by the collar and me by the arm and guided both into the house.

She shut the door in Melody's face.

"It's been like that all day." Chloe leaned against the door. "Well, Max, it looks like we take our walk in the backyard."

Chloe, Max, and I went through the house to the backyard. Max sniffed the fence and some shrubbery.

"I don't know what to do." Chloe started crying again.

"It will probably get worse." I couldn't help stating the obvious.

"Thanks for the encouragement."

I took more tissues out of my purse and gave them to Chloe.

"Do you have an endless supply?" she asked.

"Yeah," I said. "So you can't avoid my questions forever."

Chloe walked over to the fence and patted Max. "What do you want to know?"

"Let's start with the big question. Why didn't you tell me Jenna was having an affair with Gerard Paoletti?"

"It was none of your business." Chloe turned to face me. "And she wasn't having an affair with him." Her face tightened and her lips formed a straight line.

I moved toward her. "The evidence seems to say otherwise."

"The evidence is wrong."

"You mean it wasn't Gerard's child?"

Chloe and Max moved to another part of the yard. They both studied the shrubbery. Max lifted his leg.

"Nothing's going the way we planned it," said Chloe.

"You planned this?" I couldn't keep the surprise out of my voice.

"Let's go inside," said Chloe, matching action to words. "It's warmer there."

"Okay, but I still want my questions answered."

"I've already had this conversation with the police." Chloe took the leash off Max, washed her hands, and turned to me. "Do you want something to eat or drink?"

I sat at the table. "No, thank you."

Chloe came to sit across from me. "Jenna wasn't having an affair with Gerard," she said. "She was his surrogate."

"Surrogate?" Of course, I knew that a surrogate was a woman carrying a baby for another. But the surrogacy law in Massachusetts was convoluted and favored the person giving birth. I couldn't see either Jenna or Gerard undertaking such a risky proposition.

"Yeah." Chloe took a deep breath and leaned forward. "Gerard and Sylvia wanted another child and Jenna wanted to experience a pregnancy. It seemed a good solution at the time." Her hand made a dismissive gesture.

"At the time?"

"It was originally a business proposition. Not exactly business. I guess none of us believed that, after all the years of Gerard and

Sylvia trying, it would actually work."

"But it did." I took Chloe's hand. "Jenna got pregnant."

"Yeah. Even though the egg was Jenna's, Sylvia was so happy. She wanted another child and it's been almost thirty years since Richard, and everything seemed so good. We could be aunties and spoil the child, without parental responsibilities. Or so we thought."

"You said Sylvia was happy. What about Gerard?"

"At first, he just seemed stunned. Like he couldn't believe it actually worked."

We both sat in silence.

"Then he started saying things," Chloe continued. "Like, Richard was getting sicker and his care was so expensive, the baby would be an additional expense, he didn't know if he could cope. He had doubts about the whole thing."

"Why did you tell me that you planned to be parents? That technology was involved?"

"Gerard and I decided it would be simpler. Jenna was dead either way." Chloe rearranged the apples in the basket on the table. "Then the DA wanted paternity testing, and Gerard's DNA was in the system because he's in the National Guard, and we couldn't keep it a secret anymore."

Secrets. Secrets that came out at the worst possible time. I was hurt that Jenna and Chloe hadn't confided in me, angry that we had chosen an attorney for my son who kept this from me, and frustrated that I could do nothing to help Jenna or Chloe.

"The media outlets have been calling all day," Chloe continued. "Questions about Jenna, our marriage, and a love triangle, like I was involved in something unsavory. I'm on my last nerve. And it's frayed."

"I'd like to help," I said. "But, right now, I think I need to deal with what you told me."

"We still need to go visit Jenna's mother," said Chloe. "Will you go with me?"

"Probably," I said. "But I can't discuss that now. I need to leave." And I did.

I didn't go to my mother's home that night. My house was silent when I arrived. Magda was at work and my grounded children were probably sulking in their rooms. I was too tired, and too frazzled to bother checking. I sat down to read the diary that I'd brought back with me.

The front of the Cairo Tower has some greenery and a few benches. We walked past and bought our tickets to the top floor. The top of the tower consists of a restaurant and a viewing deck. Peta was right. You could see all of Cairo from the top. Cairo the modern city, radiating out from the tower, and Old Cairo, the Islamic part of the city, with its segments of Roman walls and ancient structures. I just stood at the top and stared.

"Beautiful, isn't it?" asked the man standing beside me. He had dark hair and eyes and wasn't much older than I was. Obviously not a student or a student/tourist, he wore polished shoes and a sports coat. I recognized his Massachusetts accent.

"Not from around here, are you?" I asked. I'd heard that phrase on planes and boats throughout Egypt, as one English speaker greeted another.

"Not a very original thought," he said. And walked away.

Even his backside looked good. I have this obsession with backsides and bums. If a man looks good from behind, he probably looks better coming toward me.

I went after him. I'd never chased a man in my life. Of

course, I'd only had sex with two of them. Dale I'd known since we were kids and we sort of fell into our relationship. Until I got pregnant and it went to hell. Richard, my Nile pickup, was just a mistake.

But I wanted to go after this man. I had visions of us meeting in airport hotels. Maybe even going to law school at Harvard. Not that Harvard wanted me; they sent me a rejection letter and didn't even offer to put me on the waiting list. But there had to be other law schools in Boston.

I caught up to him just as he was about to enter the restaurant.

"Sir, I'm sorry, we got off to a bad start. My name is Abbi. Can I make it up to you by buying you a cup of coffee?" I stuck out my hand for him to shake.

He stared at my hand, then my face. Then took my hand and shook it. "I'm Magda," he said. "Magda Amir. And I'm not from around here."

We went into the restaurant and sat at a table. I ordered coffee. Magda ordered something, in a language I assumed was Arabic.

"You speak Arabic?" I asked.

Magda smiled. He had a nice smile. It made his eyes sparkle. I thought I liked tall, blond men, but Magda's dark hair and eyes mesmerized me.

"My parents are from Egypt," he said. "I was born in Worcester, Massachusetts, but we spoke Arabic at home."

I knew it was a Massachusetts accent.

"And what about you?" he asked.

"I've lived all over the United States." I stopped talking for a few minutes, as the waiter brought our food. I couldn't identify most of the dishes Magda had ordered. Fish and rice and a bunch of other stuff.

"I don't think I have an accent," I said, after the waiter left.

"Only to someone from New England," he said. He dove into his breakfast. "How did you end up in Egypt?"

I gave him the version I'd created for public consumption. Taking time off between undergraduate work and law school, met Peta in Denmark and came with her to Egypt.

"So, no burning desire to see the pyramids? The Valley of the Kings?"

"I just wanted to get away for a while," I said.

I explained to him that my mother had dragged me all over the U.S. but that I hadn't done much international travel. Everything was an adventure.

Then came the embarrassing part. I'd offered to buy him coffee, and that would take the last of my money for the day. Buying him a meal meant taking out the credit card. He argued with me over the check, and ended up paying. Better to avoid an embarrassing scene of waiting to see if my credit card cleared.

We went back out on the observation deck. He pointed out the various boats on the Nile. Some houseboats that people actually lived in, some sailing vessels for tourists, and some working boats for the fishermen.

Then he turned to me and said, "You didn't have enough money to buy the food we ordered, did you?"

I became very interested in the boats on the Nile.

He got very close to me.

"No, I only had money for coffee," I said.

"Then why did you insist on paying?" he asked.

"I asked you. And I hoped my credit card worked."

"But, most likely, it would have been declined," he said.

Peta showed up just at the right time, looking for me. I introduced them. Magda took my name and phone number in the States. I took his. If he doesn't call, I'm going to call him.

I closed the diary. I did call Magda when I got back to the States. Then I had a huge fight with my mother when I insisted on attending Suffolk Law School in Massachusetts. She wanted me at the University of Georgia, near to where she lived back then. It was one of my first acts of open rebellion. With Dale, we had snuck around until we were caught. With Magda, I was open and forthright.

Or so it had seemed at the time. Magda hit me like a tsunami. He took over my life and we started spending all our time together as soon as I got to Boston. By Christmas break, we were living together and we got married after finals our first year. We had an anniversary coming up on May twentieth. Twenty-one years I'd been married to Magda.

I'd graduated from law school pregnant with Ashroff. My graduation gown barely spanned my huge stomach.

I was staying with Magda and my children.

I must have fallen asleep. I woke to footsteps on the stairs. Several sets of footsteps on the stairs. Three male sets and a third erratic step that didn't sound like it belonged to Pamela. I sat up. I was still fully dressed.

The footsteps continued past the room I was in.

"Go to your rooms. I have to deal with Pamela," It was Magda's voice.

Deal with Pamela. She was his favorite and seldom got "dealt with." Something unusual must have happened. I got off the bed and went into the hallway.

Pamela was on crutches. Step, clomp, step, clomp. The boys had turned toward Magda. Everyone looked at me when I opened the door.

"Oh, there you are," said Magda. "Let me get Pam settled and then we can talk."

"What happened?" I asked.

"Ballet mishap," said Magda. "I'll get her into bed, prop up her leg, and then come see you."

Magda was volunteering to take care of the children? Was I in the right house? Well, I would take advantage of it while it lasted. I shut the door and laid back down on the bed. Whatever had happened, it looked like Magda had it under control.

Magda was back in our bedroom within minutes. Had he had time to get Pam settled and prop up her leg? It would have taken me longer, I would have talked to and comforted her. This was a good time to try my new outlook on life. He had done the child care responsibilities, the children were safe and not complaining, let him do it.

"What's going on?" I asked. "What happened to Pam? Where did all of you go? And why didn't you wake me up?"

Magda pulled off his shoes. "One question at a time. Pam has a sprained ankle because she tripped and forgot to spin at ballet. Ashroff and I went to see Attorney Paoletti and the call about Pam came there. We went to the hospital. Somebody let Phillip off later." He pulled off his other shoe. "I don't see how you keep up with all three of them. I'm exhausted."

"Why didn't you call me? I could have helped."

"I thought you were on your way to Keene," said Magda. "And I thought it was important to get the kids back into their routine."

I'd forgotten to tell Magda I was coming back to Meredith. I needed to get better at making and keeping lists.

"Then the call came about Pam falling at ballet." Magda laid down on the bed next to me. "The last few hours have been spent in the hospital. She has a cast, and some anti-inflammatory, and she'd doing okay now. I also talked to the lawyer about Ash. We'll go to court and the charges against Ash will be dismissed. But now that all the kids are occupied, maybe we can have some alone time."

He reached for me.

WEDNESDAY

I WAS BACK IN KEENE FOR THE PLANNING MEETING ON MY mother. Dale arrived a few minutes after I did. He put a copy of the *Keene Sentinel* on the table. The headlines concerned the city council meeting and its decisions.

"Bottom of the page." Dale flipped the paper over.

It was a short article on my mother's accident. The paper said it was a hit and run and were asking for local help. Next to the article was a blurry picture.

"What's the picture? I can barely make it out." I brought the paper closer to my eyes.

"It's from the CCTV at the American Legion. Didn't get a good picture of the driver, but he had his arm out the window and his wrist tattoo is visible. A computer enhancement is on the next page."

I opened the paper. The enhancement clearly showed the driver's arm, with an ouroboros around his wrist. "I've seen that same tattoo recently," I said.

"A snake eating its tail? Where did you see it?" Dale stared at the computer enhancement.

"It's called an ouroboros. It's a symbol of eternal life, or the cycle of life, depending upon who you ask." I suppressed the urge to continue to show off to Dale. "I saw it recently on someone claiming to be a private investigator. Stowell, I think his name was. He was here, at the medical center, the first day my mother was brought in."

"And there is definitely surveillance at the hospital."

"It may not be him." I didn't want to falsely accuse anyone. "The ouroboros is an ancient symbol and might be a common tattoo."

"The police thought it was distinctive enough to run it in the paper."

"But why would he be at the medical center? To make sure he did a good job at running over my mother?" This didn't make any sense.

"Whatever it means, I think we need to notify the police." Dale picked up his phone, dialed a number, and handed the phone to me.

The dispatcher I talked to was polite but cool. Maybe they were getting a lot of calls about the tattoo and my call was just another one to investigate. I'd done my civic duty.

People were filing into the conference room. Unlike yesterday, the professionals seemed to have finished the testing and the scanning and had a preliminary plan to offer. The medical center social worker told me that the insurance company had insisted on a plan, as my mother did not need such a high level of care. An acute orthopedic rehabilitation facility had been identified and contacted. It was in New Hampshire, near the Massachusetts border. I asked for a facility in Massachusetts, but making such arrangements across state lines seemed more than the staff was capable of. As the plan was for her to be in rehab for two to four weeks, I would have some time to set up long-term care in Massachusetts.

I arrived back at the Meredith courthouse at about two. I needed to get my act together. My cases were falling further and further behind as I took care of my mother and her needs. When that thought crossed my mind, I realized my priorities were off. My mother came first. Juggling responsibilities was making my crazy.

I'd just entered the courthouse when my temporary clerk, Robert, informed me of an emergency filing.

"Can it wait or be rescheduled? It's been a tough day."

"Attorney Montoya says no. Says it has to be heard before you make a decision on George Banks and his children."

He was waiting for me in the courtroom.

I looked around. It was after three and the courtroom was deserted except for Robert, the attorney, and me.

"Attorney Montoya," I began. "This is most unusual. Are you planning to proceed *ex parte*? The matter is in litigation, the other party needs to be present."

"No, Your Honor. This is not an *ex parte* motion. I notified Attorney Hunter and he said he would be here."

No sooner had he finished the sentence than Attorney Hunter came through the door, followed by Cally.

"How long will this take?" I made a point of staring at the clock.

"Fifteen to twenty minutes."

I knew better than to believe anything would take less than an hour. But I was wrong.

The attorneys sat at their respective tables and Attorney Montoya rose to speak.

"Your Honor, I have a Suggestion of Death."

A Suggestion of Death, in legal terms, is not what it sounds like. It means someone important to the litigation has, in fact, died.

"Charity Banks was adopted by her maternal aunt. Mr. Banks was able to ascertain this by the aunt's posting on Facebook. The aunt died last week and she has no surviving spouse. As the child needs to be placed with a new caretaker, Mr. Banks would like her returned to him."

"Where is Charity now?" I asked.

Attorney Hunter answered, "The child is with the maternal grandparents, Jesus and Freya Leary. They have filed for guardianship."

Attorney Montoya remained standing. "Your Honor, my client is simply asking for an opportunity to be heard about custody. As the legal parent is dead, he has as much right as anyone else to petition for custody. And more reason than most, as he is the father."

It appeared that a custody change was inevitable. "I am not going to change Probate Court custody at this time. Charity will remain with her grandparents. But I hereby rescind the termination of parental rights, as Mr. Banks did not have an opportunity to be heard. He will have one now." I left the bench.

I couldn't stand to be in the courthouse another minute, nor have another conversation about legal issues. I left and walked into the late afternoon sunshine. The best sign of spring, when it's no longer dark at 4:00 p.m. I sat on the stone wall outside the courthouse and looked at the tulips and daffodils. Not the smartest thing for a judge to do, but I was within sight of all the court officers at the security checkpoint. This late in the day, there were only about a dozen people out front.

I felt, rather than saw, him sit down beside me. "Are you stalking me?"

"Rather a dumb move, with security behind us." Dale shrugged. "I've got some news that might interest you."

"Have you been waiting outside the courthouse for me all day? That's creepy."

"Not all day." Dale said it as if that were the creepy part. "I know you leave from the underground garage and from here I can see it and the main entrance."

"What if I went out the secret judge door?"

"Then I'd just have to catch up with you at your house tonight."

"And we're right back to creepy."

"I'm sorry." As usual, Dale did look sorry. "But I needed to talk to you. It's about Richard Paoletti."

"What about Richard?"

"Well, he didn't make the meeting in Keene today, because he had something to do here in Meredith."

"I know that. He told us yesterday."

"So, I thought I'd call him and update him on the plan for your mother." Dale stared at the passing traffic. "When I got hold of him, he was in the emergency room."

"What happened?"

"Details are a little sketchy, but it appears he was beaten up. Quite badly. His arm is broken and he has a nasty cut on his face."

"Who did it?" I asked. "Why would someone want to hurt him?"

"As I said, details are vague. Said he didn't see who attacked him, or even how many people there were. He said he blacked out and doesn't remember much."

"That's awful." I stood up. "Thanks for coming to tell me."

"That isn't why I've been sitting on this wall for the last half hour." Dale stood up also. "It's what Richard told me."

"I thought you said he couldn't remember the incident."

"He can't." Dale took the same copy of the *Keene Sentinel* out of his pocket. "It's about this."

"The ouroboros tattoo? What did he know about that?"

"Well, I told him about that part of the meeting too. Turns out he knows someone with that tattoo and his name is Barry Stowell."

"The same Barry Stowell that came to see me at the hospital?"

"Sounds like it." Dale put the paper back in his pocket. "About five ten, fifty years old. Heavyset with salt and pepper hair."

"That sounds like him. How do he and Richard know each other?"

"Barry Stowell is a private investigator that works for Richard's father." Dale let that statement hang in the air for a few minutes.

"Stowell works for Attorney Paoletti?" I felt the dread settle in. My son's attorney was connected to the man who might have run down my mother. There had to be another explanation. "Of course, he also probably works for other attorneys too. Paoletti might have just started working with him."

"Not according to Richard. Paoletti and Stowell were boyhood friends. Stowell got into some trouble in his early twenties. Paoletti helped him clear up his legal troubles and enlist in the Navy. Stowell was in the military police, then the Meredith Police Department. Left the police department after twelve years to become a private investigator."

"Richard gave you his life story?"

"Not all of it. Some I found online. Strange that he left the PD after twelve years. No pension, no reason given for leaving."

"Maybe he just couldn't stand the job anymore."

"Maybe." Dale sounded doubtful. "But I'm going to the police anyway."

My phone rang.

"It's Chloe. I'm about to go and pick up Jenna's mother. The memory unit assistant called and said she was having a good day and I'd like her to come to the celebration tonight. Will you come with me?"

"I'm still not happy with you," I said. "But I'll go." Magda and I had discussed this earlier. I would go to the academy to support Chloe and he would stay home to see that Ash was ready for his court hearing tomorrow.

After apologies to Dale, and a promise to talk to him later, I drove to Chloe's house and she slid into the passenger seat. "I appreciate what you're doing. Even if we aren't on great terms now."

"I've known you longer than I've known Magda. You get a pass for some bad behavior."

"I said I'm sorry we didn't tell you about the pregnancy and… everything." Chloe fastened her seatbelt. "I don't know what else to do to make it up to you."

"You don't have to do anything else. Just take care of yourself and Max. We both miss Jenna."

When we got to the nursing home, Jenna's mother was alert and greeted us both by name. Chloe called her "Flo," so I did also.

"So nice to see you girls." Flo was wearing a purple dress with black stockings and sat in a tall-backed chair with a belt around her waist. "I miss Jenna already."

"Flo, we've come to take you to a celebration of Jenna's life. You remember Abbi, she'll bring you home if you want to leave early. I have to stay at the theater."

Chloe and I had discussed this in the car.

"I hate funeral homes." Flo stated picking at the blanket that covered her knees.

"We're not having it in the funeral home. The celebration will be the Academy of Music. You remember, Jenna volunteered at the shows there."

"Yes, she told me about a show she was doing when she came to see me the day before she …died. She wasn't supposed to die before me. Said she was painting scenery." Flo wiped her eyes with a tissue.

"Jenna came to see you last Tuesday?" asked Chloe. "Are you sure?"

"Of course I'm sure. She left me this." Flo pulled an embroidered bag out from under the blanket. "She told me not to let it go and to remember where I put it."

I picked up the bag. It contained something small and square. I shook the item into my hand. It was a recorder. I pressed the "play" button. Jenna's voice drifted across the room.

"It's Jenna's, she gave it to me." Flo took the bag and the device from me, put the recorder into the bag and put it under the blanket. "She gave it to me on Tuesday."

Flo insisted on taking the recorder into the car. We put a wheelchair in the trunk and transferred her into it when we arrived at the Academy of Music. The parking lot was full, but space had been saved for Chloe.

The Academy was small, but full of people. It was loud, with people talking and eating and looking at pictures of Jenna through the years. The photos started with Jenna's birth picture, taken at the hospital, through high school, her marriage, and their adoption of Max, the dog.

People got up to talk about Jenna. About her work at the theater, and her planning of birthday parties, showers, and other community events. Cally talked about how she kept everyone connected at the courthouse. I chose not to make a public statement. Cally was trying to talk me into it when Flo decided that she wanted to leave.

Flo tried to get out of her wheelchair. Chloe had used the seatbelt to keep her from slipping, so she just slipped down the chair and swore. Because of the noise level, only a few people around her realized what she was doing. After a brief consult with Chloe, we wheeled her out to my car and put her into her seat.

"I'll be back after I drop her off," I told Chloe.

"No hurry." Chloe shut Flo's door. "If we finish up before you get back, I'll text you that I've gone home."

Flo looked asleep when I got in the car. When the car started, she raised her head and said, "Chloe's going to miss Jenna."

"I expect that you will too."

"Jenna came to visit me every Sunday. And last Tuesday. She's a good girl."

I pulled into the driveway of the assisted living facility.

"Where are you taking me?" asked Flo. "Why are we here?"

"You live here," I said. "I'm bringing you back to River Woods."

"I don't live here. And who are you?"

Flo was slapping the dashboard and trying to open the door. I drove up, under the overhang, and pushed the handicapped button to open the door.

"I may need help," I said to an attendant standing outside the door.

I opened the car door and Flo swung her legs out of the car.

"Flo, please sit there until I get your wheelchair." I started toward the trunk.

Flo attempted to stand and slid down on the pavement. "Look what you've made me do. Fall down. At a place I don't want to be!" Flo's voice was loud and shrill.

Two people, a man and a woman in purple scrubs, came out of the assisted living facility. They picked up Flo and set her on the car seat. I brought over the wheelchair.

The woman squatted in front of Flo. "Flo, you know me, it's Cheryl. We're going to take you to your room. Will you come with me?"

Flo stopped shouting and nodded. The two people in scrubs got her into the chair and the man wheeled her into the facility. The woman told me that they could take it from here and it was better if I left.

Back behind the wheel, I got a text from Chloe. She was getting a ride from someone else. I headed home.

When I arrived home, Magda was sitting on the couch with the laptop perched on his legs. He was dressed in pajama bottoms and a flannel shirt, with a half-eaten sandwich on the table beside him.

"How'd it go?" he asked.

"Okay, overall. Jenna's mother didn't last long and I took her back to the facility she lives in."

"You could've called me. I would help you."

"No, I think we made the right decision. I went to the celebration of life, you stay here with Ash to make sure he's ready for tomorrow. Is there anything else we need to do?"

"No according to Attorney Paoletti. I talked to him again this afternoon, he said everything was ready to go."

"Those charges disappeared fast." I sat on the couch next to Magda.

He put his arm around me. "Sometimes it's good to be a judge."

He was right. Ash's charges were dismissed, quickly, because I was a judge and anyone involved in this matter should tread lightly. I felt slightly guilty that my position made it easier for Ash than for most young men in his position. I hadn't asked for special favors, but wasn't above accepting them when they fell into my lap.

"What's with the laptop?" I asked.

"Just researching places for your mother to live." Magda turned the screen so that I could read it. "So many choices. Assisted living, elderly housing, skilled care, memory care. It looks like we can't make a final decision until we know how mobile she is. And whether she wants to move near to us."

"I think she still believes that she can return to her house in Keene and live with Dale helping out."

"She's a tough old woman, maybe she can," said Magda. "But, in the meantime, I think we need to be looking at alternatives, in case she needs more care."

"I've got a friend, Richard, who knows a lot about local care. He's looking into things for me."

"We don't need to do it tonight." Magda kissed me.

"Good."

THURSDAY

Not sure what to do next. My clerk was still dead, and my son and daughter were still grounded. I'd made the decision to stay with my husband and to conceal my fling with Dale. It hurt my head to keep it all straight.

We all showed up at court at 8:35 a.m. I know how courts work and I knew our chances of getting a hearing, even a dismissal of Ash's charges, before ten was slim. But family solidarity is everything with a teenager. Pam and Phillip were kept out of school. Both Ash and Phillip wore jackets and ties, as did Magda. Pam and I wore flowered dresses and pantyhose. As Pam said, at least they weren't matching dresses. That would just be weird.

Ash and I approached the clerk's desk, where Attorney Paoletti was waiting for us. He moved us all off to the side.

"I can make arrangements with the clerk to have your case heard last," Paoletti said. "There won't be so many people in the courtroom at the end of the day. The downside is, it will be late in the day and everyone will be tired and cranky. Let me know what you want to do."

"Ma, I don't want to sit around all day and wait," Ash said.

"You don't have to stay here," said Paoletti. "You can leave and come back about three."

"It's not the here part, it's the waiting part," said Ash. "I want this over with."

I tended to agree with him. On a selfish basis, I had cases on this afternoon. On an even more selfish basis, his last name and mine were not the same. It would do me no harm to have the case heard early and Ash clearly wanted to get it over with.

Paoletti looked over at Pam, in her print dress and still on crutches. "What happened to her?"

"She had a mishap at ballet class. She'll be on crutches for another week."

"We'll talk about that later," Paoletti left.

Paoletti arranged for us to sit in one of the tiny conference rooms while we waited for the case to be called. Ash paced back and forth and Pam read a battered copy of *Of Mice and Men*. We waited about forty minutes, a family with little left to say to each other.

Our appearance in front of the judge was brief and anticlimactic. Ash stood next to Gerard and the Assistant District Attorney announced that the Commonwealth was not going to proceed on the charges. Judge Fong asked a few questions about the case.

"And the victim was his sister?" asked the judge. "Was she injured? Why does she have crutches?"

I felt Pam's fingers press into my arm. Though I trusted Paoletti to give the right answers, the judge seemed disturbed about the dismissal. Of course, if someone wanted to write about one judge dismissing charges against another judge's child, he would be in the crosshairs.

"There were no injuries. The crutches are from a mishap in ballet class," said Paoletti. "Mr. Amir tried to persuade his sister to go home with him. It was late and she was a freshman. They started shouting and someone called the police."

Judge Fong flipped through the papers on his desk. "It says here that his sister had been drinking. She's fourteen years old." The judge looked up. "Is that her, sitting with her mother?"

Now it was my turn to be nervous, because he was looking directly at me. I refrained from grabbing on to Pam.

"The parents have grounded both Mr. Amir and his sister." Attorney Paoletti spoke as if he fully supported our decision. "This is a family matter and the family has handled it."

Judge Fong stared at me for a few more seconds. "Case dismissed. Mr. Amir is assessed one hundred dollars in court costs."

We all went back to the conference room we'd been in before the hearing. It seemed crowded with the five of us and Attorney Paoletti. Pam kept complaining that her leg hurt and she kept moving it from place to place.

"She seems quite uncomfortable," said Attorney Paoletti. "Is she going to school?"

"Yes," I said. "But it's a struggle. Her foot gets swollen at the end of the day."

"Do you need a personal injury lawyer?"

His question made me stop short. Pam had been injured in ballet class, where injuries were part of the experience. "I don't think so," I responded. "Besides, I signed a waiver."

"We should talk about it." Paoletti took out his card. "How about I drop by tonight? Around seven?"

Talking wouldn't hurt. "Okay."

Paoletti wrote "7 PM" on the back of the card and gave it to me. Magda didn't object.

"Now, to the matter at hand." Paoletti took a seat at the table and gestured to me, the only other person still standing.

I sat and turned to Ashroff. "It would be better if the one hundred dollars were paid today, to get this entire matter over with. I'll use my credit card and you can reimburse me."

Ashroff was looking everywhere but at his father and me. "I don't have the money."

"Ash, don't be a jerk." This from Magda, who had remained silent until this point. "You'll have to take it from your car fund. Last I checked, you had almost six hundred in that account. I know it will set you back, but it's important this get paid."

Ash looked at Pam and at Phillip, still ignoring his father and me. "I only have fifty dollars in the account," said Ash.

"Fifty dollars." Magda was raising his voice, never a good sign. "What happened to the rest of the money?"

Ash just sat there, looking miserable.

"What. Happened. To. The. Money." Magda wasn't shouting, but the deliberate speech was even scarier.

"I gave it away." Ash turned away from his father, toward me. "It's okay, Ma, it was for charity."

"Who did you give the money to?" Magda was trying very hard to be rational and calm, though I was beginning to question what was going on.

Ash stood up and pushed in his chair. "I gave it to the mosque. For the Somalian refugees. I need to leave." He opened the door and was gone.

The rest of us sat in silence.

"Somalian refugees?" asked Phillip. "Why would he give money to them?"

"I don't know," said Magda. He stood up. "But we're not going to find out here."

I went to the clerk's office and paid Ash's court costs. Paoletti explained that we could get them waived, but I just wanted this whole thing over with. We drove home. Magda drove Phillip and Pam to school. It was only one fifteen and I already felt like I'd put in a full day. And I was expected at the courthouse for the afternoon session.

My first case was a motion by Attorney Valley for funds to hire a psychologist for a parenting evaluation. Attorney Valley wasn't at his best today. He looked disheveled and had forgotten his tie. The motion was *ex parte*, so he was alone at the bar. No other attorneys were present because, if the evaluation was not favorable to his client, it was attorney work product and could not be entered into evidence. It also stopped the other parties from getting a copy or even requesting one. He kept shuffling papers, and looking for things. He kept apologizing, referring to "recent events" that interfered with his ability to concentrate. As Attorney Valley had the ability to sound sincere when he was putting forth the most outrageous arguments, a talent that make him in great demand at the defense bar, I ignored him.

He stopped shuffling papers and looked up at me. "I'm sorry, Your Honor. I think everything is explained in my motion."

It was and I granted the motion.

The other matter on was the matter of Mrs. Bartolli. She had let a sex offender into her home with two young children. About six months ago, I'd given custody of both children to the Department, expecting the children would be returned to Mrs. Bartolli in short order. Six months later, they were still in care. Attorney Warner, for the mother, had filed a Motion for a Reunification Plan.

"Can we do this case on representation of counsel?" I asked this at every motion hearing that was contested. The attorneys would give their arguments and I would decide on their presentation of the case. No need to call witnesses and take up court time if the facts were not in dispute.

"I would agree to that," said Niagara Fontaine, the attorney for the Department of Children and Families. The Department's attorney agreed to this plan most of the time, as it saved time and gave the Department's attorney control over what went before the judge.

"My client would like to be heard," said Attorney Warner. "She is no longer with Mr. Ignzy and wants her children to come live with her."

This was interesting. Usually, the mother's attorney wanted to present the case, again, to have control of the facts and the presentation. She expected Mrs. Bartolli to be a good witness, if she wanted to put her on the stand. Of course, maybe she realized this would be my thinking and had no intention of calling her client.

"I will hear the arguments of counsel and then decide whether we need a hearing." This was my fallback position and both attorneys visibly relaxed when they heard me say this. The attorney for the children, Barbara Norris, said nothing.

Attorney Warner went first, as it was her motion. "Your Honor, my client is asking that the court order the Department of Children and Families to develop a plan for reuniting her with her children. They are four and eight years old and have been out of the house for over six months. Mrs. Bartolli is a widow and she works part-time as a receptionist for an insurance agent. The Department had no issues with her parenting and she never came to the attention of the authorities until Mr. Ignzy moved in with her. Mr. Ignzy is a convicted sex offender and Mrs. Bartolli, in her pain and confusion after the death of her husband, made a bad decision to let him move in. She realized, almost immediately, that she'd made a mistake. He's now been gone for four months and she has no intention of letting him back in. She is able and willing to be a good parent again. We would prefer that the children be returned to her today but, we realize it is near the end of the school year and Natalie, the oldest, would need to change schools. Therefore, we are asking for a reunification plan that gets both children home over the summer. To date, no such plan has been developed, though it is the Department's mission to reunite families."

While Attorney Warner was speaking, the social worker, Harry Waters, twice approached the bar to talk to Niagara Fontaine, his attorney. He obviously did not think sending the children home was a good idea.

"Attorney Fontaine. Would you like to make a statement?"

Attorney Fontaine turned from Mr. Waters toward me. "Yes, Your Honor, I would." She stood up.

"Your Honor," she started. "The Department has continuing concerns about Mrs. Bartolli and the men that she exposes her children to. Attorney Warner said she made a bad decision and, we agree, she did. But she did not just expose her children to a Level III sex offender, a person, under Massachusetts law, that has been found to be at a high level of dangerousness and a high risk to reoffend. No, she let this person into her home and she let him care for her children. The Department went out to her home several times to explain the danger before they came to court to remove the children. She continued to allow a convicted sex offender to live with her and her children.

"As the Department continues to have concerns about Mrs. Bartolli's judgment, and whether she will let another dangerous man into her home, we have not done a reunification plan. We are asking that she continue in counseling and finish a parenting program before the children are returned to her. As a matter of law, Mrs. Bartolli is not entitled to a reunification plan. She is, however, entitled to a trial on the merits and we would be happy to schedule that."

Attorney Fontaine sat down and Mr. Waters immediately left his seat and, again, came to the bar to talk to her. It was fortunate that there is a bar separating the attorneys from the spectators. Even so, Mr. Waters was agitated and looked like he might crawl over the barrier.

As to the matter of trial dates, Attorney Fontaine knew as well as I did that it could take six months to a year to schedule and complete a trial. These children were young and needed to be with their mother before then. I had some questions.

"Attorney Fontaine, do you dispute Attorney Warner's statement that Mr. Ignzy has moved out of her home?"

"Mr. Ignzy has not been in the home the last two social worker visits. His belongings have not been there either. According to Mrs. Bartolli, he moved out."

Attorney Warner was on her feet. "Judge, it's more than that. Mr. Ignzy has been arrested again, on an unrelated matter. He is on pretrial release and is wearing an ELMO. All his movements have been tracked electronically."

Her statement about an ELMO brought, to my visual mind, a picture of a man with a red, furry creature around his ankle. ELMO—short for Electronic Monitoring device—was the name assigned both to the red, furry creature and the ankle monitor.

I turned to Attorney Fontaine. "Is this true?"

"Yes, Your Honor. He is on a monitoring device."

"And has the probation department reported that he is in a home with children? Specifically, Mrs. Bartolli's home?"

"No, Your Honor."

I picked up the file and scanned the documents that had been filed at the beginning of the case. "So, if the Department's only concern is Mr. Ignzy, and he's not there, why not return the children?"

"Your Honor, the Department has ongoing concerns about Mrs. Bartolli's judgement and the individuals she is letting in the house."

Attorney Warner wasn't ready to sit down yet. "Your Honor, my client will allow the court and the Department access to her home at any time, without notice. They can check as often as they like."

I turned to the children's attorney. "Attorney Norris, what is your position?"

Attorney Norris stood. "Your Honor, my clients want to go home. Sooner rather than later. With their mother's boyfriend gone, I see no reason they can't be returned today."

As usual, I was going to make a decision that satisfied nobody. "I hereby grant Attorney Warner's motion and order the Department to develop a reunification plan. All counsel shall be provided a copy of the plan within thirty days."

Both Attorney Norris and Attorney Warner were back on their feet, immediately realizing the flaw in my plan.

"Your Honor," said Attorney Warner. "Please accept my oral motion that the reunification plan must have the children home within ninety days."

Now came the part where I would make everybody unhappy. "I am ordering the Department to have a plan prepared within thirty days. If you have a problem with the plan, you can bring the matter back before the court and we'll have a hearing. Next case."

Attorney Norris and Attorney Warner exited the courtroom, followed by Mrs. Bartolli and the rest.

I was alone, no more cases this afternoon. I don't know whether it was light because my cases had been reassigned or because it was a fluke. Either way, I was going to take advantage of it. I spent the rest of the afternoon in my office, preparing for tomorrow's cases.

On the way home, I realized that I had never resolved the issue of what Ash did with the money he had saved. He worked for his father on weekends and vacations and it had taken him months to save six hundred dollars. Yet he had given it all away. I support charitable giving, even did it myself. But he had talked about his car for months. I didn't understand his change of heart.

When I pulled into the yard, Ash was sitting on the front steps. I pulled right into the garage, no mountain bikes or other paraphernalia in the way. As I opened the door, something fell out of the car. I stooped to pick it up.

When I stood up, Ash was standing by my car.

"What's that?" Ash gestured at the device in my hand.

"It's a recording device. Jenna's mother must've left it in my car after the funeral yesterday." I turned it over in my hand before stuffing it back in the embroidered bag she'd also forgotten in my car.

"Hey, Mom, can I borrow your car?" Ash wasn't interested in the recorder.

I got out to stand beside him. "What part of you're grounded don't you understand?"

"But, Ma." My son towered over me. Not menacing, but determined. "I just want to go to the mosque."

"We had this discussion this morning. Just because the charges were dismissed doesn't mean you're not grounded. And I want to talk to you about giving all your money to the mosque."

"Yeah, Dad's not happy about that either." Ash had the grace, or the acting ability, to look sorry.

"Back in the house and we'll talk about this."

"Then can I go to the mosque?"

"Don't push it." I linked my arm through his and walked him into the house.

Pam and Phillip were sitting at the kitchen table, playing some game that involved cards and tiny metal pieces.

I stopped short and was almost pulled off my feet when Ash continued on without me.

"Let's go into the other room," he said. "It's quieter there."

It was only marginally quieter in the living room. We continued into the study and closed the door. I put the embroidered bag on the desk.

"Where's your father?"

"I'll go get him." Ash made it as far as the door, when Magda opened it from the other side.

"Good, we're all here. Let's talk about this morning. Ash's money and what happens next."

Both Ash and Magda turned to me as I made that statement. Neither of them moved to sit down, so I remained standing. Looked like I was going to set the agenda.

"First," I felt like my mother, ticking my points off with my fingers. "Ash, you do not end a disagreement by walking out. Especially when you are grounded. It was rude to walk out this morning and you shouldn't do it again. Do I have your word you will remain in this room until we finish this discussion?"

"I just needed to be alone. It wasn't rude, it was..." Ash's voice trailed off.

"Not here to rehash the past." I ticked off another finger, as it seemed the thing to do. "I just want your word you will stay to the end of this discussion."

"Agreed."

"Magda?"

"I'm not the one who walked out," Magda said. "Agreed."

"Now, Ash, what happened to the money that you had saved?"

Ash studied the pattern in the carpet. "I told you. I gave it to the mosque."

"Your dad gave you a job so you could save money for a car and other things you'll need in the year between graduation and college. It took you months to save that money." I ticked off another finger. The items I was ticking off weren't related, but I'd found it useful in dealing with my family. "What are you going to do now?"

"Work some more," said Ash. "I'll pay you back for the court costs. If I can't go anywhere else, I can at least work."

He had a point. At least we'd know where he was.

"I'm supposed to take Sarah to the prom on Friday. Is that called off because I'm grounded? She'll be disappointed."

"You're going to the prom?" This was news to me. "And who's Sarah?"

"Yeah, I'm sorry, I forgot to tell you." Ash didn't look sorry. "I used some of the money to rent a tux and do prom stuff."

"Where did you meet Sarah?" This from Magda.

"At the mosque," Ash replied. "She was the one collecting for the Somalian charity. She said she didn't have a date for the prom, and I told her I'd take her."

"When was this conversation?" asked Magda.

"Last month," said Ash. "Before you knew I went to the mosque and I might want to convert. I didn't know how to tell you."

I pulled out the desk chair and sat down. Ash looked from me to Magda and back to me.

"So, can I go to the prom?"

"Yes," said Magda, without even pretending to consult me. "Only so your date won't be disappointed. And you will go to the supervised after-prom party or be home by midnight."

"That's not fair." My son and the universal adolescent cry. He left the room.

"What's that on the desk?" Magda went over and picked up the embroidered bag.

"Jenna's mother said Jenna gave it to her. She must have left it in my car last night."

Magda opened the bag and turned it over. The silver recording device and two horse chestnuts fell onto the desk. He picked up the silver device. "What's on this?"

"I don't know." I took the device from him. "Flo said that Jenna left it with her. I'll get it back to Chloe."

"Don't you want to listen to it?" Magda picked up the horse chestnuts. "And what's with these?"

"They're horse chestnuts. I didn't know they were in the bag. I just saw the recorder last night."

"Horse chestnuts form in the fall," said Magda. "Though I guess they last for quite a while."

"I'm going to take it all back to Chloe." I took the nuts from him and put them back in the bag with the recorder. "And I'll listen to it when Chloe is with me."

The doorbell rang.

"It's seven, that must be Paoletti," said Magda.

Magda started for the door. I put out my hand to stop him.

"I have concerns about Paoletti," I said. "But we can talk to him and then decide whether we want to hire him for Pamela and her injury." I took my hand off his arm. "Just don't commit to doing anything until you and I have talked."

Magda nodded. "I wasn't going to make a decision tonight."

Gerard Paoletti stood at the door, juggling his briefcase and two pizza boxes.

"Hope there's actually pizza in the box," said Magda. "Supper hasn't even been started."

I wasn't taking the bait. He was home before I was, he could have started supper.

"I come bearing gifts," Gerard said. "I find conversations with teenagers always go better with pizza."

"You want Pam to be part of this conversation?" Magda asked. "You're going to be mugged, we haven't had dinner yet."

"No problem," said Gerard. "I want to talk to all of you together." He put the pizza on the dining room table.

"Let me wipe off the dining room table. Magda, would you go get the kids?" I got a sponge and a kitchen towel and cleaned off the table. Then I brought out plates and lots of paper towels. Gerard opened the box and the smell of garlic and cheese filled the dining room.

Ash and Phillip burst into the room. I heard Magda's low voice and Pam clopping down the stairs. Her clopping was more regular, less tentative. I didn't know whether she was getting better and more mobile or she was just getting better at using crutches. She entered the room and fell into an upholstered chair.

"Pam, do you want some pizza?" Gerard asked.

"Yeah," she said. "But I don't know if I can carry it with my crutches."

"I'll bring it to you." Gerard seemed to be going out of his way to accommodate her.

Pam propped her leg up on another chair.

"Hey, I wanted to sit there." Phillip attempted to lift up her leg and move it.

"Leave her leg alone," I said. "Sit somewhere else."

Pizza and paper towels were passed around. Magda and I declined a piece, sure our brood would devour the entire pie.

"So, tell me how you injured your foot," said Gerard.

Pam continued to eat her pizza.

"Pam, he's talking to you," I said. "He wants to know what happened."

"You tell him." Pam took another bite.

Gerard adjusted his chair to face Pam. "You need to tell me. Your parents weren't there."

Pam put down the pizza. "I was trying to do a leap. I tripped over a box and fell into the mirror. My face bled from the cuts, but it's my foot everybody is paying attention to."

Gerard took out a yellow pad of paper. "How did it feel? After you fell?"

"It hurt." Pam picked up the pizza and took a bite.

"I got a call and took her to the hospital," said Magda. "They took x-rays, but nothing's broken."

"Let's start at the beginning." Gerard adjusted the yellow pad and picked up his pen. "What time did this happen?"

Pam said, "Tuesday lessons are at five." At the same time, Magda said, "They called me about five thirty."

Gerard made a note.

"This past Tuesday," said Magda.

Pam nodded.

"And you were trying to do a leap?" asked Gerard. "How do you do that?"

"We line up on a line and try to leap as far as we can."

"Pam, don't talk with your mouth full."

"Ma, he asked me a question."

"Can we stick to what happened?" This from Gerard. "Where did the box you fell over come from?"

"It was a box full of costumes," said Pam. "We're going to do our spring recital. The box was big and wood and it hurt."

"I'm going to get something to drink," announced Phillip.

I looked around. I hadn't put any beverages on the table. "Phil, bring drinks and glasses for everyone."

He left the room. Pam took a bite of her pizza.

"Hey, Mom?" This from Phillip, yelling from the kitchen.

"Don't yell," I said. "Come in here and talk to me."

"No, Mom, you need to come out here. Now."

I headed for the kitchen, followed by Magda and Ash. And almost slipped on the huge puddle of water in front of the sink.

"Ash, go get rags or towels." Magda opened the doors under the sink. "And I'll go get a bucket. The pipes are leaking."

Gerard came to the door of the kitchen. I looked from him to the mess on the floor.

"Can we do this another time?" I asked.

"Of course." He started to pick up his pad, pen, and briefcase. "But can I see you outside for a moment before I go?"

I followed him out on to the front lawn. It seemed that Magda had the kitchen situation under control. He threw his briefcase in the car and turned to me.

"I need to tell you something," he said.

"About Pam's case?"

"No." He stared into the yard. I'd never known Gerard to be at a loss for words.

"About what?" I was getting impatient.

"About Jenna."

That wasn't what I expected. "What about Jenna?"

"I know you've been over to see Chloe a few times," Gerard reached out and took my hand. "Just be careful around her."

"Be careful around Chloe?" I asked. "But we've been friends for years."

"I know," he said. "That's why this is so hard."

I pulled my hand away from him.

"The call that Jenna made just before her death, to Dennis Raymond." He paused.

It took me a minute to figure out what he was talking about. Strange that he would remember the person. Or maybe he knew Mr. Raymond. "What do you know about the call she made to Mr. Raymond?"

"Dennis Raymond," Gerard said. "He's the paralegal at the domestic violence shelter. Jenna called him just before she died."

"It could've been work related," I said.

"But it wasn't."

Gerard got in his car and left.

I went back into the house to talk to Magda. We went into the den.

"I don't want to hire Paoletti to represent Pam in the personal injury matter." I decided to start the conversation with my bottom line.

"Okay." Magda shrugged.

"Just okay?"

"I'm agreeing with you. Are we going to have an argument about that?"

I took a deep breath. "Don't you want to know why?"

"It's not a big deal to me. But you obviously want to tell me." Magda sat down.

Now I had an opportunity to talk, I didn't know what to say. I paced back and forth in the room.

"I don't trust Gerard. Some things he's doing and saying don't add up." I paused to gauge Magda's reaction. His facial expression remained the same. "He was involved with Jenna and she agreed to act as a surrogate for his child."

"I know that."

The surprise must have shown on my face.

"It was in the newspaper," Magda continued. "He admitted to it after the paternity test."

I got out a pen and a yellow pad of paper. "I'm going to make a list of everything we know about Paoletti, then make a decision."

"He used Jenna as a surrogate, he lied about it."

"Or just didn't admit to all the facts. I don't think I want an attorney that doesn't admit to all the facts."

"It sounds like you've already decided not to hire Paoletti." Magda paused. "Oh, yeah, that's how you started this conversation."

I put the yellow pad in front of me.

"We're going to make a list?" Magda's mouth almost twitched into a smile. "Just to play devil's advocate, I 'll argue why we should hire Paoletti."

I put a line down the middle of the pad. "Okay. On the negative, he wasn't forthcoming about Jenna."

"On the positive, you always told me he was a good lawyer." Magda tapped the positive side.

"But he lost his temper at the going away party. Attacked Rodgers when he suggested he wasn't a good lawyer."

"He attacked Rodgers? The older court officer?" Magda asked.

"Maybe attacked is too strong a word. Rodgers made a remark, like at a roast, about how he wasn't living up to his potential in juvenile court and he was moving on to ambulance chasing. Gerard lost it, saying he was always a good lawyer and tried hard. It was strange."

"Strange because your definition of a good lawyer is someone who's always in control of the situation?"

I looked at Magda. He did know me well.

"Back to the positive side," Magda continued. "He did well by Ash and Pam seems to like him."

"And I like his son," I said.

"Are you listing his positive attributes now?"

"I don't want to do this now." I threw down the pen. "And I still haven't called Chloe about the bag Jenna's mother left in my car."

I called Chloe and she agreed to pick up the bag at the court-house before she went to work the next day.

I went back into the house and picked up my diary. I hoped that reading about past times would calm me down and help me deal with the present.

Magda and I went out to dinner at a Lebanese restaurant this evening. He told me it was a different cuisine, but I didn't notice much difference from the other restaurants. But he seemed happy. He walked me to the hostel through an area filled with small shops. I told him that the shop on the corner was never open, I'd been checking. He asked why I was fascinated with that shop and I considered not telling him. But it seemed harmless enough. In the window of the shop was a burnt orange dress that represented, to me, the ideal combination of Egypt and high fashion. It had a low neckline, which was unusual for Egyptian fashion. It was tight on the top with a flowing skirt. It had a gold and green inlaid sash down the front. I said I'd fallen in love with the dress, so it was a good thing the store was never open.

We turned the corner and, at ten on a Wednesday night, the store was open. The dress was in the window, outlined in soft light from below. Magda insisted that we go in. I'm not sure I'm ready for him to buy me clothing. But I tried on the dress and it fit me perfectly. I protested that I needed to travel light and had no room for the dress in my luggage. He said he would send it to an address in the U.S. He bargained with the woman who owned the shop and got it down to a price that I could afford. I tried to pay but Magda took the dress and said that he would ship it to me.

I now owned the orange dress I had been dreaming of.

I closed the diary. I still had the orange dress, though I had worn it only a handful of times in the last twenty years. What my young eyes had seen as exotic, I now knew to be cheaply made and of a rayon-like material. It pulled in all the wrong places when I wore it too long. But I couldn't bear to throw it away. Even if it wasn't what it seemed at the time.

FRIDAY

THE CLOCK IN MY CAR SAID 7:30 A.M. WHEN I PULLED INTO the parking garage at the courthouse. I needed to catch up on my work and I didn't want Chloe to be held up so that she would be late for the start of the school day. My phone rang as I turned off the car. Chloe was parked on the street. We met and I went to hand her the recorder.

"Can we go inside?" she asked.

"Sure, I have a pass that opens all the doors. Why do you want to go inside?"

"This is probably the last thing recorded by Jenna." Chloe placed the recorder on her car. "I want to listen to it, but I don't want to be alone."

"Let's go into a conference room, sit down, and we can listen together." I picked up the bag and put it into my coat pocket.

"It's probably nothing." Chloe hesitated. "Maybe a shopping list or a message to her mother."

"But it is Jenna's," I said. "And I want to listen to it with you."

Chloe went directly to the table and sat down. It didn't seem that she was going to make this happen.

"Do you want coffee or something else to drink?" I asked.

"No, let's just get this over."

I turned the bag over and the recorder and the two horse chestnuts came out on the table.

"What are these?" asked Chloe.

"They're horse chestnuts. The nuts come out in the fall, but they were in the bag when Jenna's mother left it in my car." I turned the nuts over in my hand.

"Where would Jenna's mother get horse chestnuts?"

"I don't know." I looked at Chloe. "I thought they were probably Jenna's. Horse chestnuts are not a common tree, according to my sources."

"I didn't even know they were horse chestnuts," said Chloe. She played with the recorder. "Let's hear what this says." She pressed the "play" button.

Jenna's voice filled the room.

"Gerard says that he's changed his mind. He thinks he doesn't want to be a father at his age. You'd think he would have considered that before spending all this money to get me pregnant. Says Richard's care is getting more expensive, they can't afford another child. He didn't think this would work anyway. Fifty-year-old eggs and old sperm. Doctors said the chances weren't good, but he did it to please his wife. Both of them were surprised as hell when it worked."

The tape made a noise, as if Jenna turned it off and then clicked back on again.

"So, what am I gonna do? Even after just a few weeks, this little guy has become part of me and I want to see him or her grow up. But I'm not sure Chloe is ready to become a parent. We could do traditional gender roles. I could be mom and she could be dad. Wouldn't that be a hoot? Oh, fuck, I don't know what I'm going to do. Chloe's sister wants to have a baby, maybe they can adopt this child. Fuck, I don't know what I'm going to do. I need to think about this. Think about how I'm going to tell Chloe. Whether I'm going to tell Chloe. I could just get the abortion and tell her I miscarried. But that doesn't seem right."

Chloe clicked off the machine. "I told Jenna that, if the Paolettis didn't want the baby, we would keep it. She said she didn't want me to sacrifice for her. We argued about it just before she died."

"That hurts, doesn't it?"

"Damn right it hurts." Chloe slammed the recorder down on the table. "And now I'll never get to discuss it with her."

I didn't have anything to say to that, so I said nothing. I went over and put my hand on her shoulder. Chloe turned around and cried on my shoulder. She was a tiny woman, only about five two. It was like comforting Pamela. I just had to stand there and let her cry.

After a few moments, Chloe stepped back and took a tissue from the pocket of her pants. "Sorry to get all sloppy on you. The whole thing has been confusing."

"No need to apologize. I know it's hard." I stepped back to give her room.

I was not going to cry.

Chloe put the tissue back into her pocket.

"That's not the end of the recording," I said. "Are you ready to hear the rest?"

"Let's hear the final recording."

"I don't know what to do." Jenna's voice sounded more subdued, more ragged. Or maybe I was just reading into the situation. "Chloe says she wants to keep the baby. Because it means so much to me. Nothing said about what she feels. Maybe I should just go away and have the baby by myself. I've screwed up so many lives. Not witness protection, but maybe there's a place where I can go to be off the map for a little while. Sort things out.

"But first I need to go tell Gerard. It's his child too. He wants me to have an abortion, said having the child around would be too hard on him. He doesn't seem to care what I feel. I'm going to talk to him tomorrow morning, we're supposed to meet and decide what to do."

The tiny machine clicked. Chloe went over, picked up the recorder, and put it in her pocket. "That's it. That's the last entry."

"Did Jenna go to talk to Gerard?"

"I don't think so." Chloe stared out the window. "She never told me she went." She turned to face me. "Unless she met him the morning she was murdered."

Neither of us spoke for a few minutes.

"I'm taking this recording to the police." Chloe picked up the silver device from the table. "Now." She left.

The bag and the horse chestnuts remained on the table.

A knock on the door. It was a security officer, saying that a Richard Paoletti wanted to see me. I followed the officer the dozen steps from the conference room to the security checkpoint. Richard had been through the metal detector and was leaning on a cane. A cut on his cheek looked deep and red. The security officers were examining his scooter.

"All set." This from the officer examining the scooter. He must be new; I didn't recognize him.

Richard got back on his scooter and came over to me. "Can we talk in private?" he asked.

I led him back to the conference room I had just vacated. I pushed some chairs aside and he maneuvered his scooter into the small space.

"What's with the horse chestnuts?" He gestured towards the bag and nuts on the table.

"Just another matter I'm pursuing." I pushed them to the side.

He leaned over and picked them up. "They're from the trees in our yard."

"How can you tell that by looking at them?" I asked.

"Horse chestnut trees are not common. There's only about a dozen in all of Meredith." He turned over the horse chestnuts. "But these have been marked." He showed me a V-shaped mark in the lighter center of both nuts. "My father carries around horse chestnuts, year-round. Says they help his arthritis. And he notches them to let out the healing energy. He learned that from his father."

Paoletti was at the center of this. He hired Jenna as a surrogate, Jenna planned to meet with him, these appeared to be horse chestnuts he'd handled and Barry Stowell was an investigator who worked for him. No direct evidence, but enough to go to the police.

Richard was waiting for me to say something.

"Are you sure they're his?" Not a brilliant question, but important.

"Let me tell you why I came to the courthouse this morning." Richard put the nuts back on the table. "I knew you'd see me, because of your mother, but I'm here because of this." He touched his cheek, the one with the deep gash on it.

"It does look nasty."

"My father hit me. Not for the first time." His statement hung in the air.

My phone pinged. A text from Chloe: *Dropped off the recording. Police are investigating.*

I texted her back: *Learning more about Paoletti. May be dangerous. Stay away from him.*

Richard was still waiting for me to say something.

"I'm sorry," I said. "What can I do?"

"I'm not going back to the house. My bag is packed and in Dale's car. I was hoping I could stay in your mother's house, with Dale, until I figure out what to do next."

"What to do next?"

"Yeah, I've never lived on my own. And I'm scared to death I won't be able to do it. Dale will help me with finances, medications, personal care attendants, and all the other things I need to schedule and figure out. I'll pay you rent."

"You don't need to pay rent." It sounded altruistic, but I knew I could get him out of the house at any time if he was a guest, not a tenant. Damn, my legal caution was working even in charity work.

"So I can stay in your mother's house with Dale?"

"My mother won't be home for a couple of weeks. You'll need to make other arrangements by then." What was I getting myself into? I'd figure it out later.

"What the hell is going on?" The voice came from behind me. I turned to find Attorney Paoletti standing in the doorway.

The unknown court officer was standing behind him. "Sorry, Judge," he said. "He pushed past me. Do you want me to escort him out?"

"No," I said. "But contact the local police and Trooper DePaul of the state police, and tell them that Mr. Paoletti is here."

"Yes, ma'am." He turned to leave.

"And leave the door open," I said.

Paoletti turned to Richard. "What are you doing here?"

Richard said nothing.

"Leave the room," said Paoletti to Richard. "I want to talk to the judge alone."

"No." Richard sat up straighter in the seat.

Paoletti turned to me. "Are you setting my son against me?"

"I think you've done that yourself. He says you caused the cut on his cheek."

"He lies." Paoletti glared at Richard.

I took a deep breath. "I want to talk to you about Jenna. And the baby."

"I've already talked to the police," said Paoletti. "What do you think you can find out that they don't already know?"

"I spoke to Dennis Raymond, the man Jenna called just before she died. She said she was afraid of somebody and she may need to hide now. Did she talk to you about this?"

"The last time I talked to Jenna was the weekend before she died. As I told the police, she wanted to talk about her options." Gerard got up and moved around to the back of the couch. "That was the last time I saw her."

"No, Dad, I think you made a mistake." This from Richard, still on his scooter in the corner.

Everyone turned to look at him.

"I don't think I made a mistake," said Gerard. "I talked to her that weekend."

"Jenna said she was on the way to meet with you the day she was killed." Not strictly true, but close enough.

"She didn't make it because I didn't see her," Gerard said.

"When did you tell Jenna you'd changed your mind?" I asked.

"I didn't tell her I'd changed my mind. I said circumstances had changed. We discussed options." Paoletti took a few steps inside the room. "Is this why you want the cops here? Because of some half-baked conspiracy theory you have?"

"I don't think it's half-baked," I said. "Jenna was your surrogate, she said you were having second thoughts, she went to meet you, and she died."

"And then there's the horse chestnuts," Richard said.

"Horse chestnuts?" Paoletti turned to look at him.

"Yeah, horse chestnuts," echoed Richard. "Notched with a knife."

Gerard started pacing back and forth. "And what is the significance of horse chestnuts? I hear they help with arthritis."

"There are only about a dozen horse chestnut trees in town," said Richard, "and eight of them are in our yard."

I remembered admiring the trees the first time I went to his house. I thought they were majestic but didn't realize they were horse chestnuts.

"When did you become such a horticulturist?" This from Gerard, in a monotone.

Everything went still. I didn't even hear anyone breathing. Then Richard let out a long sigh, as if he had finished a hard task.

"What are you accusing me of?" asked Gerard.

"Of being the last person to see Jenna. And lying about it." I said.

The silence piled up in the corners. Richard started a few "but," and "okay," sentences, but never went any further.

"I'm a good lawyer, so I'm going to stop talking now," said Paoletti.

"That may be a good idea." Trooper DePaul had arrived.

Paoletti turned to face him. "What are you doing here?"

"Judge Hartwell asked for me. I wanted to see you anyway."

"About what?" asked Paoletti.

"I want to talk to you," said DePaul. "About a recording, by Jenna Jay, implying that she was on her way to see you around the time of her death."

"Implying? A recording you can't authenticate? Doesn't sound like good evidence to me." Paoletti crossed his arms and leaned on the table.

I told the trooper about the horse chestnuts and the marks on Richard.

Paoletti continued to stand with his arms crossed. "My son told the hospital that he fell off the scooter. And horse chestnuts don't mean anything."

"Mr. Paoletti, I'd like you to come with me to the station, for questioning."

"For questioning? I'm a respected attorney and my reputation is what I sell to my clients. How will it look if they know I've been taken in for questioning? I'm a pillar of the community, I contribute to local charities, and I'm on the board of the Y and the hospital. You'll need more than speculation to bring me in."

"Sir, I'm only asking for a few hours of your time. Or we can take you to the station."

"You'd love that, wouldn't you? Take down a prominent local attorney. No way. Am I under arrest?"

"No, sir."

"Then I'm leaving." Paoletti went to the door. "I'll discuss this with my lawyer and tell you how I'm going to proceed." He walked away.

"What's going to happen now?" asked Richard.

"As a judge, I'd say the District Attorney has a pretty decent case. Circumstantial, but decent. Of course, they are still waiting on DNA evidence, fingerprints, and the other high-tech stuff. Only on TV do they get results in a few days."

"And I'm going to take the new evidence to the DA. See if we can go forward. Can I recommend the DA come to you for warrants?" Trooper DePaul smiled.

"Conflict of interest doesn't begin to describe where I am," I said. "You'll have to take your chances with another judge."

"My dad is angrier than I've ever seen him." This from Richard, who hadn't moved.

I'd forgotten that Richard had a personal stake in the outcome. Gerard was family and Richard needed to deal with him. "I'm glad you're not going back to the house. You need to keep yourself safe."

Richard turned to face me. "But my mother's there. She may need to be protected."

"Your mother didn't protect you. She had to know that your father was hurting you."

"She tried to protect me," Richard said. "She couldn't, when Dad got going. My dad had a hard life, with a disabled son and doing District Court work, with clients that often didn't pay him. Then he got the personal injury recoveries and he had money. We bought a van for me, with Stowell to drive, and a larger house, all on one floor. Dad got paid regularly and he was good at negotiating with the insurance companies. They were going to have another kid."

"Then what happened?" This from Trooper DePaul.

"Then Dad decided he didn't want another kid, he wanted to enjoy his new life. He joined boards and gave to charities and got his name in the right places. He even joined the country club, though he hates golf. Now it looks like he may lose it all. I don't know what he's going to do."

I remembered Paoletti at the going away party. He was proud of his new life and lashed out at anyone making fun of it, even in jest.

"I'll give him a couple of hours to calm down," said Trooper DePaul. "Then I'm bringing him in. I'll need to get statements from the two of you also."

Richard left the room, followed by the trooper and me.

SATURDAY

I READ ABOUT GERARD PAOLETTI'S SUICIDE IN THE MORNING paper. He'd left a note, saying that his wife and his son had nothing to do with Jenna's death. He'd shot her, but it was an accident. He'd only wanted to talk to her and brought the gun as protection. The article was short, devoid of facts, and chilling.

Magda put a cup of coffee in front of me.

"I spent hours last night at the police station, giving statements to three different officers. Got home after midnight and fell into bed." I gestured toward the open paper. "And then there's this."

Magda sat down across from me. "Did you know about this last night?"

"No." I took a sip of the too-hot coffee. "But I suspected it wouldn't end pleasantly."

"You should read the information online. It makes you out to be the judge who took down a murderer."

I felt like such an imposter. I didn't take down a murderer and I couldn't save Jenna.

"And Dale called," Magda continued. "He said that the New Hampshire authorities are talking to Stowell about his part in your mother's hit and run."

"Did he make the call that got her out on the road that day?"

"Don't know. That investigation is still open." Magda stood up. "Do you want something to eat?"

"Just toast. I'm not feeling well."

Magda put bread in the toaster and sat back down.

I took a deep breath. "Magda, what would you think if I tried to find my daughter, Heather?"

"What brought this on?"

"Richard kept talking about his family. Despite everything that went on, he was still worried about his mother. And he wants to meet his biological sister. He's taking chances I've been running away from."

"And you think finding Heather would help?" Magda stood up and brought the toast, butter, and marmalade to the table.

"I don't know. But I'd like to find out more information than I have now." I pushed the toast away. "I don't think I want to eat."

"You need to eat something. Eggs? Protein shake?"

"I said I'm not hungry." Why did he keep bringing up food?

"You know I'll support you in whatever you want to do." Magda reached out and took my hand. "I made a doctor's appointment for you today at ten. Figured it's a weekend, I could go with you."

"I don't need to see a doctor. I'm fine. I just don't want to eat."

"You don't think I noticed?" he said.

"Noticed what?"

"You're a week late. Only been late twice in the twenty years I've known you. Once with Ashroff and once with the twins."

"I'm not pregnant," I said.

ACKNOWLEDGEMENTS

This book includes some firsts in my writing career and I know the new people have made this a better story. Thanks to Stillwater Press and Steve Porter. This is my first project dealing with this press and they made the process understandable and, at times, enjoyable. Many, many thanks to my new critique group, Bodies in the Library, who patiently read my less-than-best work. I do appreciate the work put in my Mary Ann Faughnan, Mary Small, and Betsi Tennessee, who did her best to make me stop repeating myself.

As always, my beta readers, Diane Kane and Robin Shtulman, were indispensable.

My family has stood by me and encouraged me through this endeavor. This book is dedicated to my parents, who made me believe I could do anything. And thank you to my son, Tony; his wife, Tina; and their children, Abbi, Alex, and Brent. They demonstrate courage and explore new possibilities on a daily basis.

Made in the USA
Middletown, DE
13 March 2020